School Daze

by William Siems

School Daze
Copyright © January 2024 by William Siems
Published 2024 by William Siems

ISBN: 979-8-9900413-0-1

First printing - Spring 2024
Scripture quotations from the SUV (Siems Unauthorized Version) of the Bible

Contact the author at chayeem10@gmail.com

Cover by Jacob Bridgman
Artwork by Gil Henry (used by permission)

Interior design by Alane Pearce of Pearce Writing Services LLC
AlanePearceCoaching.com/contact.

Dedication

I thought I would write a novel. It took forty-five years. Its sequel came much faster (forty-five days?). Since then it has been about a novel each year. While in the middle of a series about following an archangel down through the ages, I stumbled on this one, a departure from the norm. So, here it is, "School Daze." Again, without the faithful support of so many it still would have remained a stumble. Thanks again to my wife, Nancy, who was my constant inspiration and encouragement, and most importantly to the editing of my daughter Angela. She edits with what I would call brutal compassion. She also tries to keep me on track theologically (good luck with that, says the guy who wrote his own gospel). Then, of course, thanks to the center of the whole thing, the Promised One, Jesus.

Table Contents

Prologue

Grover Cleveland High School is rather unremarkably located in the suburbs of Franklin, a medium sized city. It does reap some of the benefits of its location. Franklin's economy includes a large, stable middle class of both blue- and white-collar workers involved in the textiles industry. The two divergent classes seem to get along most of the time. The school is well-funded and has weathered many of the recent turbulent times with grit and determination. The people believe in the value of a good education, and it shows in their response to every bond issue.

Their commitment goes beyond the three R's of reading, writing, and arithmetic. They have had state contenders in baseball, basketball, and football for the last five years, as well as being largely recognized for the sports of tennis, track, and golf. They also strongly support the classes of language, literature, history, and the sciences. They even added the soft sciences of Psychology and Life Skills to their curriculum a number of years ago. They are fortunate enough to employ one of the few full-time teachers of those two subjects. Over the years, Nick Grant has been closely associated with the total excellence that Cleveland High delivers and he is one of its most beloved teachers. His classes would always be filled beyond capacity if it were not for the school's strict adherence to state guidelines.

Tonight is the first Parents and Teachers Association (PTA) meeting of the school year. Mr. Benson, the school principal, steps up to the podium.

He smiles broadly, "Welcome to our first PTA meeting of this school year. I have asked Pastor Tom Tuttle to share our invocation. Pastor?" He stepped back from the podium as Pastor Tom rose from his seat and stepped up to it.

"If you are new here, you may find it odd that we begin in prayer, but prayer is just conversation with Him," and he pointed upward. "It does not require that you bow your head or close your eyes, although some people do that to help them focus. You can just talk to Him as though He were here," now Tom was smiling broadly, "because He is." He began, "Thank You for the opportunity to get together as parents and teachers at the beginning of this new school year. Help our meeting to be both effective and efficient as we work together to raise these kids. Thanks, Amen." There were a chorus of other 'amens' followed by a single raised hand in the middle of the seating.

"I thought it was no longer legal to pray at school," a well-dressed man stated.

Pastor Tom had been replaced by Mr. Benson again. "That is a normal misconception and concerns only compulsory prayer. We can't 'force' your children to pray. An invocation or benediction at a meeting is a 'different breed of cat,' so to speak."

"Thank you for the clarification," the man responded.

Mr. Benson continued, "Now, as always, it is my pleasure to introduce a man who doesn't need to be introduced to most of you, Mr. Nick Grant." There was light, but prolonged applause as Nick rose and stepped up to grasp the podium.

"I am pleased to announce that this is my tenth year at Cleveland," and he was interrupted by more applause. He raised a hand, and it quieted down. "Your kids are our top priority, and you know that we don't take the task of helping you raise them lightly. I am privileged to help them understand themselves a little better and assist them in grappling with some of the skills they will need to master in order to have a full and successful life here in the Franklin community. As teachers in your high school, we dedicate ourselves to that task with renewed vigor this year, and remember, if you ever have any questions or comments, we welcome them all. Thank you." More applause accompanied Nick's return to his seat.

Mr. Benson began, "You should have a copy of our agenda before you. We don't have too many things to cover tonight, but let's get right to it. First…" and for the next forty-five minutes there were some short presentations and spirited discussion.

Pastor Tom concluded with a, "Thank you all," he gestured to the crowd and then pointed upward, "for a productive evening. There are cookies and beverages for those of you who would like to linger and speak with any of us personally. Thank you again, you are dismissed."

Coffee in hand, Nick spoke with a couple of parents when a woman joined them with a, "Ten years?"

Nick smiled; he did that a lot. "Mrs. Janders. Yes, it is hard to believe. I think I even get your youngest this year."

Mrs. Joyce Janders returned the smile, "And I expect the same wonderful results I have found with the first two."

Nick returned, "As far as it is up to me, you shall have them."

The friendly banter continued with her and others until it was time for them all to say good night.

Nick walked to his car with the usual spring in his step. He anticipated another great year.

Chapter One:
Nick and Ann

Nick and Ann met in college. Nick had been at a private college for three years on a partial scholarship in music. He played both the saxophone and the clarinet, and was quite good, scholarship good. He had not added the flute to his musical tools yet but was considering it when it was announced that tuition would be raised again the next year. He transferred to the state university and that's where he met Ann, and everything changed. He hadn't felt that he was cut out for a career playing music. He had tried some gigs and had enjoyed them, but it was a pretty wild life and he didn't appreciate all the trappings that seemed to go along with a music career. Instead, he had begun to focus on education. Maybe he would teach music, but he soon realized that while he liked to play music he did not really like to study and teach it. That was when he took his first psychology class and fell in love with it, and soon with her.

She sat on the other side of his Abnormal Psychology class, and he noticed her glancing in his direction a lot. A couple of times when their eyes met, she smiled.

He caught up to her after class, "You either took really poor notes today or have a very strange habit of glancing in my direction for concentration." He continued, "Whenever I glanced your way, I found that it broke my concentration concerning Mr.

Stroble's lecture, not enhanced it." As she smiled, he realized she had dimples. Had he missed that before?

She took her time in answering him. He wasn't sure if that was a good or bad sign. "The answer to your question is, yes. Normally it would enhance my note taking to glance in your direction if it was just a direction. That was before I realized you sat over there." She might have been blushing at that point. It was difficult to tell with her tan.

"Could I interest you in a cup of coffee or tea?" he asked with anticipation.

More dimples, "Yes," and they walked to the Student Union building. She had neither coffee nor tea. She didn't like either one. She just drank hot water. He found that more interesting than odd.

The following week Ann asked Nick if he would like to drive her over the mountains to a friend's wedding that next Saturday. It would be a long day; over in the morning, wedding in the afternoon, reception, and then back that night. He said, "Yes!" without hesitation.

He surprised her by showing up in his father's sports car, the silver convertible. The top was up, but once they got over the pass, they pulled over and put it down. It was a gorgeous sunny day. It was a large Episcopal wedding, very 'high church,' except that the groom sang to his bride before their vows. There was hardly a dry eye left in the place. The ceremony was followed by a formal dinner in the late afternoon. Then they began a beautiful drive back, starting with the top still down, but turning the heater on full bore as they climbed the pass.

At the summit, they stopped for a fast-food snack, put up the top, and sat at a picnic table outside the fast food joint while finishing their milk shakes. Nick slipped off his seat, got down on one knee and said, "Ann, will you marry me?"

Ann's response was instantaneous, "What? Are you crazy? You don't even know me! We have been together two weeks and you're asking me to spend the rest of my life with you?"

Nick got up and sat back down on the bench. "I guess that's a 'No,' huh?" and then went on like nothing had happened. Ann could hardly believe it had really happened, except for the rest of the school year he would ask her to marry him about once each week.

Finally he wore her down and she said, "Yes, if you can get my father's blessing." She knew that would be a formidable task. Her dad had scared the socks off most of her other potential boyfriends.

However, after he had first met Nick, her father had said, "He's not very intimidatable, is he?"

"Hmmm, was intimidatable even a word?" she had thought.

After she had provisionally said, "Yes," Nick took her father aside that next weekend and said quite candidly, "I would like to marry your daughter, but I want your blessing."

Nick was pleasantly surprised at the response. "Her mother and I have talked and prayed about this," and he paused to let him sweat a little. "You have our blessing."

That night, as he left, they walked hand in hand to his car. He opened his car door, turned to say good night, but said instead, "Your father gave me his blessing to marry you." She almost fell over, then jumped into his arms, and kissed him tenderly.

Chapter Two:
Preparing

Nick's final year at university began with his student teaching. He was extremely fortunate to teach at Grover Cleveland High school. They were just adding a Psychology Department to their strong academic curriculum, so he was able to cut his teeth on teaching with what had become his favorite subject.

On the first day of class after Nick introduced himself, he began, "Personality, what is it?" He looked around the room. No one had raised a hand. They didn't know this new teacher yet. "It might be said that personality consists of all the things that come together and uniquely make you, you," and he paused for a minute. "But what if we could make some generalizations that would help us understand one another?" Still no hands. "There have been many attempts to assess personality. The Myers-Briggs assessment came out in the 1940's and though widely popular, identifies 64 kinds of people. While interesting, it is way too complex to remember or for most people to find useful in their daily life. I am an IFTJ, what are you?" Again he looked around the classroom, no hands, then began again, "There are a number of four quadrant systems that I have found both simpler to remember and to use effectively. So, we are going to take a test." He noted their shock, "No, not a test, an assessment. It is thirty questions that will help you determine which of the four categories best describe you and your behavior." He pointed to two people in the front row, "Judy and Jon, could you help me by passing out the assessments for me?"

While initially shocked that he knew their names, Judy and Jon stood, took the papers, and passed them out. During the fifteen or so minutes that it took for the students to fill out the assessment, Nick walked among them and handed out another piece of paper face down.

"Now, if you will turn over the other sheet of paper that I just passed out and follow the instructions on it you will be able to assign your answers to each question into one of the four personality quadrants, then total the answers for each quadrant and see which one contains the most of your answers. For the rest of the quarter we will assume that is your quadrant. All right, check your answers." Once they had completed that task, he had them gather their materials and move to the quadrant in the class that contained the most of their answers. The Deciders moved to the front left of the class. Behind them were the Detailers. Next to the Detailers were the Dancers, and in front of them, the Dreamers. When the students had moved to the quadrant their answers had indicated, he proceeded with the rest of the lesson.

That weekend, he and Ann attended a pre-marriage conference at one of the larger congregations in the center of town. The lectures, assignments, exercises, and small group sessions were all excellent. They had read the book beforehand and fully immersed themselves in the information and its process. It covered gender differences, their version of personality typing, finances, communication, intimacy, and a dynamic relationship with Jesus Christ, all the things that normally get in the way of a healthy marriage and what you need to build instead. Much of it they had already covered from reading the book and doing the exercises in it, but this provided a safe atmosphere to explore things further and go even deeper. They wanted to take advantage of every opportunity to make their upcoming marriage incredible, and it was working.

The wedding plans were all coming together. They would be married shortly after graduation. The high school had offered Nick a part time job when he finished his student teaching, building the curriculum and classes that he would begin full time in the Fall. Things were falling into place so wonderfully that it was hard to believe. They felt blessed with special favor from God as they prepared to begin life together.

Chapter Three:
Teaching Ten Years Later

Nick taught a young people's Sunday school class each week for years at Franklin Christian Assembly, a mid-sized interdenominational congregation. His class was well attended and his lessons much appreciated each week.

He began, "This morning we are in John chapter eight. What can someone tell me about this chapter that is unusual?"

Four hands were raised, "Christy?"

Christy spoke clearly and confidently, "The first part of the chapter is not in the best Greek manuscripts."

There was Nick's smile again, "Which means?"

Christy returned his smile, "That the story it contains might have very well happened, or not, but was added later."

"Correct," and Christy now beamed. Nick continued, "So, here's the story from the GUV, my favorite translation." The GUV was the "Grant Unauthorized Version," his own and was between a translation and a paraphrase. Plus, he sometimes added some extra-biblical material to the story. Rumor had it that he was actually writing his own version of the gospel and there was a lot of anticipation to read it.

"John chapter eight," and he began to read the text:

> While being a courtesan to the rich and influential
> had advantages like clean beds and customers,

usually, the profession itself remained the same: stroking men's egos with pleasure. Whatever Ahlam had been looking for when she had begun this journey, she had not found it and still searched. She sat mulling over the nagging emptiness of life, her life. She had comfort, a measure of safety, plenty of nice things, but she lacked an elusive something. Maybe it was purpose, a powerful reason for being. Janus cared for her, almost like a father, and now she had Marie to look after, but what was the meaning of it all? One day just followed the next. There must be more.

She heard a soft, but insistent, knock at her door. A client this early in the day would normally be unusual, but it was not. As a priest, he needed to be more circumspect than most. They had seen each other before, and she thought she knew what to expect. She was dreadfully wrong.

He had only been there for half his usual visit when a sudden flood of scribes and Pharisees suddenly poured into her bedroom. They seized her, gagged her, bound a robe around her, and carried her from the house into a large mob of people. They dragged her along with them, barely allowing her to keep her feet. As she looked around, she saw many of her regular customers caught up in the malevolent passion of the moment. Fear rose in her throat threatening to choke her. Her place of business lay near the temple and the momentum of the crowd carried her in that direction. "What could this mean?" The roughness of her handling and the jostling of the crowd knocked off her gag and loosened her bonds, but fear held her tightly in place and she could only weep. She could feel her tiny life swallowed up in the murderous rage of this crowd.

Jesus had come to the temple that morning, and a crowd gathered around him. He had taken his usual seat on the temple steps. Many of the crowd also sat, so he began to teach them, as he often did.

Suddenly, around the corner came a mob of people. Led by the scribes and the Pharisees, they dragged a woman with them. They brought her to Jesus, then thrust her forth to stand alone. She wept softly. Slowly Jesus stood to his feet.

"Master," coming from their spokesman it sounded like a thinly veiled taunt, "this woman was taken in adultery, in the very act!"

Jesus thought, *"And how did they accomplish that, collusion?"*

The spokesman continued with exaggerated deference, "In the Law, Moses commands us to stone such a woman to death, but what do you think we should do?" He gripped a stone in his hand, ready to begin the gruesome spectacle, and said this to test Jesus. Jesus had made a mockery of the Pharisees, driving their money changers and animals out of the temple, saying he would rebuild the temple in three days. They intended to expose him as a fraud, but they needed some concrete evidence against him. With this women they saw their chance. The Pharisees knew Jesus had escaped other verbal traps, *"But let's see him get himself out of this!"* The words screamed in the Pharisee's head.

Jesus looked at the crowd, then at the woman, then knelt, and began to write something on the ground. He listened to his Father as he wrote *"You shall love the Lord your God with all your heart, soul, mind, and strength..."* As he did this, they continued to pester him for an answer. Finally, he stood up and said quite calmly, "He who is without sin may cast the first stone." He knelt back down, listened some more, and slowly continued to write, *"and you shall love your neighbor as yourself."*

The oldest of the Pharisees, even more revered than their spokesman, stepped forward, a rock in his hand. Ahlam saw all of this through her tears. She knew what came next. She prepared herself as best she could. The Pharisee looked down at what Jesus had written, the words Jesus had said ringing in his ears. He hesitated, thinking, *"Surely, I should be the one to throw the first stone."* He looked again at what Jesus had written. Guilt engulfed his heart, remorse for what he himself had done. With the picture of his own sin emblazoned on his mind he let the stone fall from his hand. Ahlam flinched at the sound of it striking the earth. The Pharisee turned, walked silently out of the courtyard, and left the temple. The eyes of the crowd followed him as he left. The spokesman stepped forward, fiercely grasping his stone, only to find his heart similarly gripped by the guilt of his own sin. He dropped his stone and left. Ahlam flinched again as it hit the ground. One by one, each of the others stepped forward to experience their own form of regret and let their stone join the Pharisees'. After a while, Ahlam quit flinching as the stones clattered to the ground, hitting one another. Soon all the mob, even those he had been teaching, had gone, leaving him alone with the woman, who still braced herself for the impact of the first stone that would hit her.

He stood up and stepped towards her and reached out to take her chin in his hand. Startled out of her fear, she looked into his eyes as he lifted her head. He dropped his hand, "Woman, where are your accusers? Does no one condemn you?" Why did he call her, "woman" she wondered. Surely even he had heard of Ahlam, the famous palace courtesan. He could have called her any number of other things. Perhaps he did not see her as just the object of men's desire, a toy to be used and cast aside. Perhaps he saw her as simply a woman, a lost, hurting woman.

A spark of hope glimmered in her soul.

She looked around while she dried her eyes on the sleeve of her robe. No one stood around her any longer, no one to condemn her. She stopped looking and dropped her head again. He remained. He could condemn her.

He reached out, lifted her chin once again, and she looked into the eyes of the purest, most powerful love she could have possibly imagined. "Neither do I condemn you," he said. "Go, and sin no more!"

The spark burst into a flame, *"Go and sin no more? Was that even possible? Could I really begin a new life, from this moment on?"* As he let go of her chin and then brushed the back of his fingers against her cheek, he simply nodded. "Yes." She felt more power in that unsaid word than in all the armies of heaven.

She turned to walk away, filled with a love and a purpose she had not dared to believed existed moments ago. The hope of a new possibility-filled future motivated her with a love beyond words. Fifty steps away, she turned back to look at him. He still stood there, looking at her and smiling. The next time she turned around and looked, he had gone.

"So, what stands out to you from this story?" Nick asked the class. A number of hands were raised. "Let's start with you, Doug."

Doug stood, "The religious leaders were trying to expose Him as a fraud."

"Why would they want to do that?" Nick countered.

"Because He threatened their way of life, the status quo," Doug added.

"Yup, He did that. What else?" Nick looked around, "Ted?"

"They were within the law to stone her. She had been caught in the act of adultery," Ted said slowly.

"And what about what he wrote on the ground?" Nick grinned.

"We don't know what he wrote. You added that," Ted replied confidently.

"True, we don't know what He wrote, only that it and what He said stopped them in their murderous tracks," he said satisfied.

Meredith spoke out, "Why didn't He condemn her? He could have."

"Yes, He could have, but He did not come into the world to condemn the world, but…" and Nick left the sentence unfinished.

A number of them finished it for him, "to save it!"

"Yes," and he went on, "the healthy (or supposedly healthy) have no need of a physician, only those who are sick. He came to call sinners to repentance, not the righteous." Nick's pleasure in his class was obvious.

It was Ted again, "But He didn't call her to repentance."

"What did He say to her?"

He said, "Neither do I condemn you. Go, and sin no more!"

"And was that adequate for this situation?"

Ted nodded, "So it would seem."

"As we have often found, we do not live by rules, formulas, etc. How do we live?" Nick looked around again and began to smile again as he saw Walter raise his hand, "Walter?"

Walter spoke sheepishly, "By every word that comes out of the mouth of God?"

"Yes, or as Jesus put it in another instance, 'I only do what I see the Father doing.' That is how we are to live. Well, that's about it for today. Walter, would you close us in prayer?"

Walter looked like he just swallowed a frog, but spoke out, "Thank you for today's class, but mostly for your example of how

You followed the Father in everything. Help us to do the same. Amen."

There was a chorus of other "Amens," and Nick dismissed the class. A few of the students hung around and asked him some follow-up questions, all which he graciously answered. He took so much time with them that he entered the morning worship service in the middle of the second song.

Ann and the girls were standing in their normal place as Nick straggled in. The girls came out into the aisle, and each hugged him as he passed by them to stand by Ann, They finished the next three songs and then sat down for the announcements and offering. The kids were excused to 'children's church' when the congregation stood and greeted one another. As the commotion died down and the congregation retook their seats, Pastor Tom stepped up to the podium that a couple of the guys had moved front and center on the stage.

Nick woke with Ann squeezing his knee. He'd dozed off? He hoped no one else had noticed. He looked at Ann who shook her head slightly. Tom's messages were usually mesmerizing not hypnotizing. He took out his notebook, maybe that would help him focus. Why was he so tired? It had been a difficult year. His mother had died of a heart attack, followed closely by his brother who had died of a lymphoma form of cancer. More recently, his dad had been diagnosed with pancreatic cancer and quickly succumbed about two months ago. They were a definite example of "bad things can happen to good people." The cumulative effects had probably exhausted him emotionally. He didn't feel tired but must be more tired than he felt. He made it through the message without dozing off again.

As they rose and were dismissed, Ann leaned over, "I lost you for a minute there." She smiled.

Nick smiled back weakly, "I didn't drool or snore, did I?"

She chuckled softly behind her hand, "Not this time."

Chapter Four:
Tragedy Strikes

Betty, the school secretary, knocked on Nick's door and entered at his, "Come in?" Looking at her he asked, "Betty, how can I help you?"

Betty looked sheepishly around the classroom before she responded, "Mr. Benson would like to see you in his office. I will watch over your class in your absence."

Abe spoke up from his seat in the front, "Uh oh, Mr. Grant. He found out about our next psychological experiment." The class twittered with laughter.

Nick smiled, "Well if he did then we have a pretty good idea where the leak originated."

Abe piped up again, "Well, his daughter is in this class," and left it at that.

However, Mr. Grant looked at Abe more seriously. "Helen would rather swallow her textbook than betray us," he said confidently. Helen sat taller in her chair, smiling. "Now, excuse me for a few minutes. Betty, my lesson plan is on my desk. Abe, keep things on track until I return. Ladies and Gentlemen, you have your assignment," and he left the classroom.

Mr. Benson, the principal, had an office at the end of the hall. Nick walked casually down the hall. He was in no particular hurry. While he loved his students and the courses that he taught, a short break in the action was always nice. He even stopped for a drink at the water fountain between the boys' and girls' bathrooms. A little bell attached to the top of the office door tinkled as he entered.

Mrs. Hill lifted her head to see who had entered. Nick spoke softly, "Mr. Benson is expecting me." An interesting looked passed over Mrs. Hill's face. It seemed sad, which was uncharacteristic of her. She was generally quite upbeat.

"Go right in," she also spoke softly, then weakly smiled.

Hmmm, interesting, and he opened Mr. Benson's office door. There was a police officer in the office, who turned around, Officer Hadley. "Tom," and Nick reached out his hand.

Tom took his hand and held it, "Nick," there was a look of concern on his face, "take a seat." He let go of his hand.

Mr. Benson stood, came around his desk, and stopped next to Officer Hadley. They looked at each other wondering who should speak. Finally, Mr. Benson spoke. His tone was low, slow, and he seemed to be choosing his words carefully. "There has been a tragic car accident. Your wife and daughters have been killed."

Suddenly, there was no air in the room. He closed his eyes, bowed his head into his hands, and waited. He prayed silently for strength. Ever so slowly there was air again and sound.

Mr. Benson was speaking, "Take as long as you need, Nick. We'll find someone to cover your classes for as long as it takes."

His lungs finally full of air again, Nick sighed, lifted his head to look at Officer Tom Hadley and Principal Hugh Benson as he said, "Thank you." He took another deep breath. "It's Tuesday, let's see, for the rest of the week my lesson plans are pretty explicit. Do you remember Al Gunderson, the student that taught with me last year? He was incredible. If you could get him to fill in for me that would be excellent. That would give me a few days to pull things together and then I can call you over the weekend with an update."

Both men were awed at how well he was taking this. He noticed their shock and smiled albeit weakly, "You know the old saying 'they are in a better place?' It is true. It won't mitigate my loss or grief at losing them, but it does help in this initial moment." He took another deep breath, "Let me go back and let the students know and then I'll be back, and we can finalize a plan, okay?" Tom and Hugh looked at each other and nodded. Nick reached out his hand again to Tom, "Thanks again." Then to Hugh, "I'll be right back," and he turned and left the room. The two men were still somewhat bewildered.

Nick stepped back into his classroom and it was like he had never left. Everyone seemed occupied with their assignments, and all seemed to be in order. Betty sat in his chair at his desk.

They all looked up as he entered. Although he didn't need to say it, he said it anyway, "Let me have your attention for a minute." They gave it to him. He took another deep breath to steady himself, "There has been a tragic accident, my wife and daughters have been killed." There was a collective gasp, but he continued, "I'm going to take the rest of the week off. Abe, if you could please monitor the rest of the period."

He quickly responded with, "Yes, sir."

"You will have a substitute for the rest of the week," and he smile weakly, "I expect you to be really nice to them." There was a general nodding of heads. A boy in the middle of the class raised his hand, "Yes, Jack?"

Jack stood up, "This might not be appropriate, but could I pray for you?"

A lump began to form in Nick's throat, "And I probably shouldn't say, yes, but," and he made a hand gesture for him to continue. Two gals also slid out of their desks and all three of them knelt right there on the classroom floor.

When Jack was through there was hardly a dry eye in the class, including Nick's. He mumbled, "Thank you. I hope to be back next week," tore that period's lesson plan out of his book and handed it to Betty, grabbed the rest of his stuff, and left the classroom.

Chapter Five:
The Next Day

Still reeling with the revelation of yesterday's tragedy, Nick sat at his favorite table, in his favorite chair, at his favorite Chick-fil-A, and awaited his order. He wasn't really hungry, but he needed something to occupy his hands as well as his mind right now.

Julie, one of his favorite servers, although he didn't really have favorites, brought him his breakfast.

He mumbled his normal thank you as he looked up to find tears in her eyes. She stepped close to the table, put down his order, and uncharacteristically reached over and took his hand. One tear fell on the back of his hand, "If there is anything we can do, anything at all, you have but to ask." It was obviously much more than just words.

A lump formed in his own throat, "Of course," and he smiled weakly. She let go of his hand, stepped back, and turned slowly back to her serving. He bowed his head for a moment, and he prayed a little more deeply than usual, "Thank you for this food," he touched his breakfast, "this place," he touched the table, "and these people," and a single tear slipped from the corner of his own eye.

He heard the front door open and looked up. His table and chair had him looking directly at the front door and if he looked to his left, the side door too. He was the unofficial breakfast greeter and knew the few regulars who came in each morning, shortly after the restaurant opened. This, however, was not one of the regulars. He was an older man, at least he looked old, but there was an air of virility that seem to emanate from him almost like a fragrance. His eyes met Nick's and he smiled. Nick nodded in acknowledgment and the man stepped towards the counter and out of Nick's view.

Nick looked down to his regular chicken, egg, and cheese muffin and tater tot hash browns. He wasn't sure he could handle them today, but he opened the tater tots and sauce anyway.

Before he got to the muffin, the old man stepped up to his table, tray in hand. "May I join you?" he asked without insisting. It was clear that Nick could decline, but he did not. He nodded towards his table. The man set down his tray, pulled out his chair, and sat with a smile.

Nick smiled weakly in return, "I haven't seen you here before."

The man shook his head slightly, "Nope, first time, but I like it. Nice place, nice people, now we'll see about the food," and he bowed his head for a moment. Nick left his eyes opened but bowed too.

"You're a Christian?" Nick asked.

The man smiled even more, "I could have been speaking to Allah." Nick looked down, sorry for his assumption, as the man continued, "But you are correct, although the term has some unfortunate connotations now days. 'A follower of the Way,' it was called in the beginning."

Nick's smile began to grow. This man's presence was pleasantly cheerful and engaging. "I sit corrected," Nick said, even laughing a little.

The man had opened up his biscuit, but reached his hand out across the table, "Jonathan," he said.

Nick took his hand and the picture of a gift all wrapped up in a beautiful ribbon, ready to be opened, flashed in his mind. "Gift" that was the Hebrew meaning of Jonathan, "The Lord gives," Nick responded. "Nick, from Nicholas, but only my mother called me that," he paused, "when I was in trouble."

Jonathan smiled as he released Nick's hand, "And are you in trouble, now?" What an interesting question. It caught Nick totally off guard. Seeing his consternation, Jonathan followed with a light hearted, "Just kidding." That helped, but not totally. There was still something nagging at his subconscious.

Nick sighed, "Not that kind of trouble."

Jonathan responded quickly, "I didn't mean to…"

"That's okay, you couldn't have known," he sighed again. "My wife and daughters were killed in a car accident yesterday by a drunk driver."

"Oh, I'm terribly sorry," and his concern seemed genuine. Jonathan reached out his hand again. "Take my hand again."

Nick scowled questioningly as he looked at Jonathan's offered hand, but before he realized it, he had taken his hand again. He looked up into Jonathan's eyes.

"Take a slow deep breath," it didn't seem like a command, but neither did it seem something that could be ignored. Nick took a slow, deep breath holding Jonathan's hand. "Another." He looked down at the hand, back up into the eyes, as he took another slow deep breath. "Last one." Nick took one final slow deep breath and realized something, somehow had changed deep within himself. "Hope," Jonathan said, "in despair. It's still there," and sure enough it was there. Deep in his soul Nick could somehow, now, feel hope. Jonathan released Nick's hand, picked up his chicken biscuit, and took a bite. Much of it crumbled back into the wrapper.

Nick actually smiled, a real one this time, "They're a bit crumbly, but really good."

"Yes, they are," Jonathan mumbled with his mouth full.

Strangely relaxed, Nick said, "Yesterday was the morgue, funeral arrangements, and a lot of heart-rending phone calls."

"I can only imagine," Jonathan responded.

"You've lost someone close?"

Jonathan raised his palms off the table, "Been around a long time," and he paused. "I could make a few suggestions if you'd like."

"Sure," and something passed between them. He wasn't sure what it was, just something. "That would be helpful."

"Grief has its own schedule. Don't be in a hurry to get out of it or get over it. It's just a process you need to walk through. It is easier if you can walk through it with someone. Do you have someone?"

Nick looked down at the table, "Hmmm, probably no one like that. Well, Jesus, but..." and he left the sentence open.

Jonathan seemed to understand. "It needs to be Jesus with 'skin on,' if you know what I mean."

"Someone I can touch, yeah."

Jonathan continued, "I'd be willing to help if I may."

"No offense, but we just met."

"None taken, but sometimes that can even be an asset." Jonathan reached into his shirt pocket, took out a small case of what looked like business cards, selected one, and passed it to Nick. "Will you be here tomorrow?"

Nick smiled, "Yup, breakfast, six days a week."

"Okay, I'll check in tomorrow." He finished his biscuit, picked up his drink, "Do they do free refills?"

"Yes, they do."

"Okay, see you tomorrow," he tipped his cup and walked towards the counter.

Nick looked at the business card. There was a small target with an arrow right in the middle and the caption, "Getting to the heart of things," his name, Jonathan Graham, and a cell phone number.

Just before he walked out the door, Jonathan turned to Nick, put his other palm next to his cup that was held in his other hand. While awkward, it still looked like a gesture of prayer. He pointed to Nick, and then left.

"*What an interesting fellow,*" Nick thought.

Chapter Six:
The Next Day at School

Normally, second period was the first period that Mr. Grant taught each day. Today, as students filed in for class, they had a substitute teacher, as Mr. Grant was away on bereavement leave. A young man sat at Mr. Grant's desk. On the white board was written, "Mr. Gunderson."

Kids filed in and were all in their seats when the bell rang. It was pretty remarkable, but Al Gunderson remembered when he had taught here last year. Even then he was greatly impressed with both Mr. Grant and the way he conducted his classes. It had been a great, even eye-opening experience for him. He had jumped at the chance to substitute for him, even though the circumstances were sad. He couldn't even begin to comprehend the pain and grief Mr. Grant must be experiencing.

Al stood, "As the board says, I am Mr. Gunderson, I know, it's a mouthful to say when you are used to getting by with just Mr. Grant, but you'll do okay. I've taught for Mr. Grant before, he's left me a great lesson plan, and I am familiar with his style. I can't replace him, but between us we can do well enough that he won't have to worry about his classes while he's gone. I'm sure you all know about the tragedy. We are collecting funds for his favorite charity, "Rescue the Children." There is a container on the desk if you would like to contribute sometime this week. Questions?" One kid in the middle of the class raised his hand, "Yes?"

"Have you talked to him? Is he okay?"

"No, I have not talked to him personally, but Mr. Benson assured me that he is doing as well as can be expected under the circumstances. Many of you, perhaps most of you, know that he is a Christian, but there is still the pain of loss to work through. He should be well supported. Please keep him in your prayers. Now, today we begin his section on personal finances." Al was expecting a groan, but there was more of an aura of expectation. *"Wow, what a privilege to teach here,"* Al thought. "So, why learn personal finances?" A student in the middle of the class raised his hand. Mr. Gunderson recognized him with, "Dennis?"

Dennis was initially shocked that Mr. Gunderson knew his name, but recovered well, "You may have a dream, but if you can't finance it, it's more just a hallucination."

Al smiled, "Well said, Dennis." He paused, "In order to have the best and most efficient personal finances there are some foundational beliefs that I would propose. Number one: have no debt, zero, nada, none."

Sandi raised her hand, "Mr. Gunderson, how is that even possible?"

Al scrunched his face up a bit, "A good question, Sandi. Zero debt is the goal, but it may not always be achievable. It would be closely followed by another: If you have to get into debt, get out of it as soon as possible."

She raised her hand again, "But don't I need to incur some debt and pay it off in order to achieve a good credit score?"

Sandi had obviously been doing her homework. Al responded with a chuckle, "Sandi, why do I need a good credit score?"

Sandi came back quickly with, "To make major purchases on credit."

"And incur more debt? Hmmm, seems like our culture has an agenda here." He had a bottle of water on the desk which he opened as he said, "I know it almost seems unAmerican to have no debt. I mean isn't capitalism fueled by buying more? Ah, but do I have to buy on credit? With good financial planning as part of my personal finances, I can limit the need to buy on credit, and hence the need for a good credit score." He took a drink and sat on the edge of the desk, "So. Where do we start?"

A hand shot up in the front, to which Al responded, "Alice?"

"The budget?" she said.

"Is that a question?" he smiled.

"The budget," she stated emphatically.

"That is correct, the budget. A budget designed to get and keep us out of debt. What other functions should the budget serve?"

This time Carl raised his hand, "Yes, Carl."

Before he answered the question, Carl asked, "How do you know all of our names?"

"Well, Mr. Grant left me a seating chart and in his class, his students would all tend to sit in their same seats. Pretty simple, huh?" Al was still grinning.

"But when did you get his seating chart for this class?" Carl was still a little mystified.

"I picked it up yesterday after Mr. Benson asked me to take his classes."

"And you have memorized the seating charts for all five of his classes?" Carl sounded more mystified.

"Yes, and why would I do that? Do you realize that calling you by name is the second most loving thing I can say to you? Just think of how special you already feel just because I know your name." Carl nodded. "The only more loving thing I can say to you, Carl, is, 'I love you' which isn't appropriate in class." That got a few twitters. "Now back to the questions. Besides getting and keeping you out of debt what other functions should the budget perform?"

Carl found his voice, "Assuring that you don't spend more than you earn."

"Yes, expenses must be less than income. Good! So, how do we assure that?" Al asked.

A guy in the back raised his hand, "Yes, Jacob?" Jacob looked puzzled. "Yes, I know that you and Joe switched seats this morning," They looked at each other wide-eyed. "and now you think I might be psychic. No, but I did notice your looks to each other when I mentioned the seating chart." Mr. Gunderson's status was soaring. While they were going to miss Mr. Grant, they were beginning to realize that his classes were not going to suffer one iota under Mr. Gunderson's direction and instruction. "Now, how do I know what my expenses are?"

Karen hadn't raised her hand yet, but now she did. "Kitty, I know the chart says Karen, but you go by 'Kitty.'" Her jaw dropped. He gave her a moment.

Finally, she recovered, "You keep track."

"That is correct. You start keeping track, keeping receipts, until you can build a monthly budget and revise it a few times until it works for you. You will categorize the expenses, like, how many of you have a car?" Six hands went up. "You might have a car payment, annual insurance (divided by twelve), gas, maintenance, etc. all in the 'automobile' category." He looked at the clock on the back of the wall. "Think about what other categories there would be for tomorrow's class, and don't forget the jar on the desk if you want to contribute to Mr. Grant's favorite charity. See you tomorrow," and the bell rang.

Chapter Seven:
The Day After at Home

Yesterday had been difficult, but Nick assumed it was just the beginning of the difficult things. Identifying the bodies had been rough. At least they weren't mangled or disfigured by the accident, just dead. Of course, as a Christian, he didn't see death the same way that Western American culture did. While it was the end of an old chapter, it was also the beginning of a new one, just not in the same place. The really difficult part was the loss of them being there. Even so, everywhere he looked, he still saw them or at least reminders of them.

Fortunately they had prepaid arrangements with a mortuary, so that was one less worry. Then there were all the phone calls. He had switched to carrying his African phone, the one he used a number of times while on mission in Africa. It was a separate number, and he wouldn't be inundated by callers, most of whom were sincerely concerned, but right now a distraction. He had left a new voicemail message on his regular phone, "You have probably heard about my loss. I will be taking a few days away and have switched to my African phone. If you need to contact me, my pastor and my principal have that number. Otherwise, leave a message, and thanks for your prayers."

Then there were the calls that he had to make. While his family were all already gone, his mom to a heart attack, his dad and his brother both to cancer. While Ann's parents were gone due to a sickness they had contracted while on mission to Africa themselves, there was still her older brother, and Nick had called him. He had also called his pastor, Tom, who already knew, so that would take care of the church network. Later, he had sent an email out to a few others. Finally, he set the memorial service up for two weekends away. Ann's brother and that group of friends were all from out of town and there were other arrangements that he needed to coordinate to pull that off well.

Some might think it odd that Nick and his wife had spent a weekend away together planning both of their memorial services, but it sure made things easier now. Their will and finances were also both in order, so that helped too. He did, after all, teach personal finances to his high school students and he lived what he taught. That was one of the many reasons that his students loved and respected him.

Nick lived in a small three-bedroom home in the suburbs. When they had the second daughter, they had decided to let them share a room. Ostensibly it had been to let him use the third bedroom for an office, but that took a long time to materialize. It kept being used for some other purposes. They housed visiting missionary couples who were home on furlough on a number of occasions. Their daughters loved the people and new experiences that it brought into their lives. Then there were the college-age kids. They had provided a home away from home for both single guys and gals over the years, some who had become like extended family. Two of them, both wonderful singers, were slated to sing at Ann and the girls' memorial. It would be really special.

Mr. Benson had called him yesterday and assured him that Al Gunderson was going to pick up his classes for him. That relieved the burden of worry about his classes. Al was a great young teacher and would deliver his classes with both wit and excellence. The prior year, when Al had done his student teaching with Nick, it had been a hoot. It still brought a smile to Nick's face even amidst the current pain of his loss.

He sat before his computer on the breakfast table, a cup of decaf beside his laptop. He was reviewing the memorial service that he and Ann had designed for her, in case she passed first. Who would have thought he would lose both her and his daughters at the same time. A tear formed and trickled down his cheek as he reviewed the event they had designed. He looked over to his left and his heart nearly stopped. There sat Ann in her usual spot reading her devotions. He could hardly breathe, he just looked. Finally, she looked up at him and smiled, "We are okay, you know that. Still, I'm sorry we had to leave you. We love you." Those words echoed in his kitchen until he broke eye contact to look back down at his keyboard, his eyes filled with tears. He looked back up. She was gone.

He sighed and looked back to the memorial service they had put together. He would email it to his pastor, Tom, later. They had already spoken, so Tom was expecting it. He hoped it would serve as much more than just a memorial service. He hoped it would change people's lives.

Chapter Eight:
Mr. Gunderson Teaches

M r. Gunderson sat at Nick's desk as his students filed in talking and laughing with each other. When the bell rang, they all sat and quieted as Mr. Gunderson stood up and walked around his desk. "Mr. Grant has given you some initial instruction about personality and I believe you took a short assessment that put you in one of four categories?" There was a lot of head nodding. "How many of you remember your category?" All the hands in the class went up. "I would like you to get up and move to your category, Deciders up here," and he pointed, "Detailers behind them, Dreamers over there with Dancers behind them." George raised his hand, "Yes, George?"

"Mr. Gunderson, I scored the same in two categories. Where should I sit?" he asked.

"George, what were the two categories?"

George smiled, "Detailer and Dancer."

Mr. Gunderson smiled too, "What's the square root of one hundred and twenty-one?"

George leaned over and asked the gal next to him, stood back up and answered, "Eleven."

Mr. Gunderson's smile broadened, "Sit with the Dancers please." George moved to the Dancer section.

Mr. Gunderson moved up to the whiteboard and drew the four quadrants and labeled them. "Now, look at the people in the quadrant diagonal to you. Deciders, look at Dancers, Dreamers look at Detailers. If there are some people that you have difficulty with in that quadrant, raise your hand." Quite a number of people raised their hands. "In your own quadrant, talk amongst yourselves about why you have difficulty with the people in the diagonal quadrant. Assign someone in your group to take notes. I know, Deciders and Dreamers, you don't normally take notes, but this time make an exception and have someone take notes." Al sat down and there was the buzz of conversation for the next fifteen minutes.

Mr. Gunderson got up from his desk and stepped around it. "Deciders, why do you have difficulty with Dancers?" Norma stood up, "Yes, Norma."

Norma smiled. She was still surprised that Mr. Gunderson knew everybody's name, including hers. She turned and looked at the Dancers then back to Mr. Gunderson. "Without mentioning any names," there was a twitter of laughter, "they are really slow at making decisions because they are trying to be sure everyone is happy with the decision." A number of the other Deciders nodded their heads. "They don't get anything done 'cause they are always chatting." There were more nods.

Mr. Gunderson smiled, "Anything else?"

Norma continued, "They are always interrupting us, about this thing or that. Send an email, a text, post a sign, we'll figure it out, but don't bother us. We're trying to get stuff done."

"Thank you, Norma," and she sat down. "Dancers, I know it's hard for you to say anything bad about anyone," more twitters, "but what difficulties did you come up with that you have with Deciders?" Alice stood up and he responded to her standing, "Alice?"

"Mr. Gunderson, they are cold, aloof, impersonal, uncaring, unemotional, demanding," she took a breath, "pushy, and quick to make decisions based on hardly any data at all. They tend to be arrogant, self-centered and self-absorbed. Should I go on?"

Mr. Gunderson laughed, "I think that's good for starters, Alice. Thank you. Detailers, how about your problems with Dreamers?" Judah stood up. "Yes, Judah."

Judah picked up his notebook, "Do you want them ranked in the order of how offensive they are?"

Mr. Gunderson laughed, "No, that's not necessary, although I'm sure you could do that." Laughter still colored his voice.

Judah began, "Dreamers, as their name implies, seem to have little relation to reality. They are flighty, moody, and sometimes just plain 'off the wall.' They think they are funny, but often they are just silly or inappropriate. They seem to exist in their own little world, and it is an alien one. They make decisions based on no data at all. In fact, they make the data up to support their decisions. Their logic is hard to follow, and it is probably a stretch to even call it logic. That's just this side of the paper. Do you want the rest?"

Mr. Gunderson smiled at Judah, "That's fine, thanks. Finally, Dreamers, tell us what bothers you about Detailers." Marshal stood up. He did not have his notebook in hand. "Marshal?"

Marshal was a frequent actor in the school plays, known for his ability to ad lib and improvise, "We don't have any problems with Detailers, much." That brought chuckles from most of those in his quadrant's group. "They are difficult to work with because they think they are always right. Well, they usually are, but anyway," more chuckles from his quadrant and a quick, "So do you, but you aren't!" from the Detailer quadrant and them chuckling. Marshal continued, "They are either reclusive or cliquish. We know that you can make a good decision with about eighty percent of the data collected. They always want one hundred and twenty percent of the data. How can you even collect that? Collect some of it twice? They suffer from analysis-paralysis and tend to find fault with everything. Is that enough?"

Mr. Gunderson smiled, "Yes, that will do for now, thank you Marshal." He looked around the room. "Great job on the negatives, or the weaknesses of each quadrant, but let's look now at their positives, their strengths." He stepped up to the whiteboard, grabbed a black marker and drew a vertical line from near the top of the board to near the bottom of the board. Then across the middle of the board, bisecting the vertical line, he drew a horizontal one of equal size.

Decider	**Dreamer**
Decisive	Enthusiastic
Goal-oriented	Visionary
Powerful	Spontaneous
Competitive	Optimistic
Daring	Inspiring
Assertive	Humorous
Thorough	Relational
Predictable	Empathetic
Dependable	Helpful
Orderly	Harmony
Careful	Loyal
Punctual	Team-player
Detailer	**Dancer**

He labeled the four quadrants and asked the students to try and turn the negatives into positives for each of the quadrants starting with the Deciders until he had the chart filled out.

"Great! I'll see you tomorrow," and the bell ending class rang.

Chapter Nine:
The Breakfast Test

Nick sat at his favorite table, eating his favorite breakfast, at his favorite place, Chick-fil-A. He got up to get a refill of his drink and rounded the corner to the order desk. There was a single customer standing there. The man had a gun in his hand and looked at Nick as he walked up to the counter to set down his empty cup.

The man spoke shortly, "Put your cell phone on the counter and return to your seat and you won't get hurt."

Nick smiled at the man, "Put your gun down and come talk to me and we'll tell the police there was a misunderstanding."

The man looked menacingly at the cashier, "You called the police?"

Nick responded, "No, she didn't. There are silent alarm buttons all over. Someone else has probably initiated it, but we'll let them know that it was in error. There is also an alarm on the safe. She can't open it. Now, put the gun down and come talk to me, please."

The gunman looked confused. He looked at the cashier, at Nick, through the window to the kitchen, and back to Nick. He slowly lowered the gun and started walking towards Nick.

Nick breathed a sigh of relief and a silent prayer as he spoke to the cashier, "Julie, when the police show up could you go out and meet them and tell them there has been a mistake?"

Julie looked at him sheepishly, "What do I tell them?"

Nick stopped on the way to his table and said, "Tell them you thought he said, 'Gimme your money,' but what he said was, 'Don't have any money,' and the menacing tone scared you."

Julie flinched, "But that's not true?"

Nick said to the man, "Say to her, 'Don't have any money.'"

The man shook his head, but said to Julie, "Don't have any money."

Nick smiled, "How's that?"

Julie seemed still squeamish, "What about the gun?"

Nick looked at the man, "Put the gun in your pocket," and he did it automatically. Nick looked at Julie again, "No gun. So, don't mention it." She just shook her head and went outside to wait for the police while Billy took her place at the counter.

Just before Nick turned the corner to his seat at his table, he called back, "Billy, could you refill my cup and bring it to me? Thanks."

Billy called back, "Sure, Mr. Nick."

Nick stood by his seat at the table and extended his hand, "Nick Grant."

The man looked at the hand and before he realized it, found his in it. He gulped, "Alfred Galipso, but my friends call me Freddy."

"Well, I hope to become your friend, Freddy, have a seat." Nick gestured to the seat across the table from himself. "Have you had breakfast?"

Freddy shook his head, no, "Do you work here?"

Nick chuckled, "No, I have just been coming here for years. I may be the unofficial breakfast greeter." He chuckled again, "And I know the combination to the bathroom. Breakfast?" and he handed him his phone open to the breakfast menu on the App.

Freddy looked at the phone and passed it back. "I'm not very phone savvy. Could you order for me?"

Nick smiled; he did that a lot. "Sure, can I suggest the chicken, egg, and cheese muffin meal?" Freddy nodded. "Tater tots?" Another nod. "What would you like to drink: coffee, tea, soda, juice?"

Freddy cleared his throat, "Coffee, black."

Nick pushed a few buttons and noticed that the police had driven up and were talking to Julie. He hit the submit button as he said, "The food will be here in just a minute, Freddy. The police have arrived, but don't be alarmed. If an officer comes in, I will talk to him."

The officer did come in and Nick stood up at his table, "Officer, how may I help you?"

The officer approached, "The alarm was activated."

Nick stepped towards the officer, looked at his badge, and extended his hand, "Officer Holmstead, I'm Nick," He stood next to Freddy, who had his back to the officer, reached back to place his hand on his shoulder, and continued, "this is my friend, Freddy. What did Julie tell you?" And he motioned outside towards the police car.

"She said it had been a mistaken call, but she seemed awfully nervous, so, I thought I should check it out myself."

Nick chuckled again, "Officer Holmstead, you are a bit imposing." Nick paused and looked around, "Everything's fine here."

The officer too looked around and then seemed satisfied. Nick offered, "Sorry for the trouble, thanks for the response."

The officer shrugged, "You're welcome," turned and went back out the door. The atmosphere relaxed. The officer got in his car, left, and Julie came back inside.

Nick spoke to her, "All okay?" She shrugged. Out of the corner of his eyes Nick saw someone enter the drive-thru. "Okay, back to business, someone just entered the drive-thru." Julie went back behind the counter and out of Nick's line of vision.

Chapter Ten:
A New Friend

Billy brought out Freddy's breakfast along with Nick's refilled drink and set it between them. Freddy looked up sheepishly, "Thank you."

Billy responded with the typical, "My pleasure," but knowing Billy, Nick knew that he meant it.

Nick looked at the tray of food and added, "I ordered some ranch sauce for the tater tots, but they have lots of other sauces."

Freddy looked at the food himself, "No, this is fine."

As Freddy reached to open the ranch sauce, Nick said, "Do you mind if I give thanks for the food?" Freddy looked back quizzically. Nick took that for a *"No, I don't mind,"* and began. "Jesus," Freddy quickly bowed his head, "thank You that Freddy gets to share breakfast with me and thanks for the food." Freddy still bowed his head. Nick finished with, "Amen."

When Freddy looked up, he exclaimed, "Who's that?" and pointed behind Nick.

Nick turned around and there sat Jonathan. He hadn't seen him come in. "Oh, that's my friend Jonathan. Would you like him to come to join us?"

Freddy shook his head, *"No."* He opened the ranch sauce, then took the tater tots, began dipping them in, and eating.

Nick began softly, "So, why were you going to rob us?" Freddy glanced apprehensively toward Jonathan. "Oh, he won't eavesdrop."

Freddy looked back at his food, seemingly shamed, "You were right. I have no money. I haven't eaten in awhile. I'm an ex-con and nobody wants to hire me."

"So, what can you do?" Nick asked sympathetically.

"Most any kind of general labor. Oh, I used to drive a forklift." Freddy had inhaled his tater tots and was halfway through his muffin.

"Hmmm, how much would you need to tide you over for a week?" Nick inquired.

Hope might have ignited in Freddy's heart as he thought about it for a minute. "Couple hundred maybe."

Nick's grin was back. "What if I could get you a couple of hundred? Would you promise me not to rob anybody for a week?"

Freddy started to grin too, "Sure, but where are you going to get a couple of hundred dollars? Maybe I should have just robbed you?"

Nick was still grinning, "Well, you wouldn't have got that much in the till and I don't have it on me, but there's a cash machine just down the street. Wanna take a walk?"

Freddy's grin was replaced by surprise, "Why would you do that?"

Nick pondered his response a moment, "Your showing up on my watch was not a coincidence and I know some folks that I think could use a good laborer. You do work hard and are dependable?"

Freddy furrowed his brow, "How do you know I won't lie to you?"

Nick nodded, "I'd be able to tell."

Freddy took a deep breath, "Sure, let's go for a walk," and began to get out of his chair, crumpling his muffin wrapper as he stood and started to pick up his drink.

As Nick got up he turned to Jonathan, "I'll be back in about ten minutes. Then we can chat." He put his drink back on the table, rounded the corner, and said to Julie and Billy, "I'll be back in about ten minutes, don't throw my drink away," and he winked at them both.

They went out the door together, down across the street to where there was a cash machine. On the way Freddy asked, "You're not an angel are you?"

Nick raised an eyebrow, "If I told you, you wouldn't believe me," and he looked at him. "No, I'm a school teacher. I teach at Cleveland High, but I'm also a novelist and I write about angels."

With genuine interest Freddy responded, "Have you ever seen one?"

Nick gave a short laugh, "Same answer," and paused, "you are right though. They can appear as just men. You might have met one and not known it." They were standing in front of the cash machine, just the two of them. "Let's say three hundred for good measure." He entered his card, password, and in a few keystrokes, he held three hundred dollars in his hand, all twenties. He held it out to Freddy, "Come back in three or four days and hopefully I'll have some good news for you."

Freddy took the money and there might have been a tear in his eye. "You're sure you're not an angel?"

"Nope, but I do believe in them. Next time I'll bring you one of my books. They're only ten dollars," and he laughed. "I'm at Chick-fil-A every morning but Sunday. We're closed on Sundays." Nick reached out his hand, "It was nice meeting you Freddy."

Freddy eagerly took it, "You too. See you in a few days."

Nick turned, walked away, and then turned back around, "You might want to sell the gun," and laughed again as he turned back and kept walking.

Freddy reached down and patted his pocket. He had forgotten that he had a gun in it, but now he had three hundred dollars in the other pocket. There was a slight spring in his step as he walked off in the other direction.

Chapter Eleven:
Back at Chick-fil-A

Jonathan had moved up to Nick's table and was guarding Nick's drink when he walked back in the door. Jonathan commented, "Pretty successful morning, all things considered."

Nick sat and took a long drink from his cup, "Nothing like a little excitement to take my mind off my troubles for thirty minutes." Nick saw Jonathan was nursing a coffee, "Have you eaten?"

"Nope, angels don't need to." Nick looked like Jonathan had just cold-cocked him, "Just kidding, but then we can just look like a normal man can't we?"

"Were you listening to my conversation with Freddy?" Then he remembered they had spoken about angels outside, on the way to the cash machine.

Jonathan smiled, "Naw, I have read one of your books though. I found it thought provoking."

Nick returned the smile, "Ah the sweet sound of success."

Jonathan retorted, "So, how many kinds of angels are there?"

Nick's eyes perked up, "Well, there are regular run-of-the-mill angels, archangels, cherubim, seraphim, what about the 'four living creatures' around the throne?"

"That's good for now." Jonathan added, "Can they all appear as men?"

"Hmmm," Nick thought a moment, "I'm not sure."

"Do they have different personalities?" Jonathan probed deeper.

"I'm not sure," Nick repeated.

Jonathan explained, "You give them different personalities in your books: Lucifer is a bit arrogant, Gabriel is somewhat wordy, R'gal is funny. Do you see my point?"

Nick smiled, "I think I'll stay with, 'I'm not sure' a bit longer."

Jonathan went on, "If they have different personalities, when they appear as men, might it not be a reflection of their real personalities?"

"Hmm, something to think about." Nick was obviously already pondering it.

"Come on, Nick. You have already thought about a lot of this. It shows in your books," Jonathan challenged.

Nick thought he would throw him a curve ball, "So, are you an angel?"

Another grin began to form on Jonathan's face, "I can answer that, but then…" he left the sentence unfinished.

Nick shook his head, "I know, you'd have to kill me."

Jonathan's grin grew, "Well, maybe not that drastic, just wipe it from your memory."

"You can do that?" Nick exclaimed.

Jonathan fully laughed now, "No, I was just pulling your leg. That's a funny expression, 'pulling your leg.' Do you know where it originated?"

Nick shook his head.

Jonathan explained, "No one really knows. There are a number of competing theories. The most prominent and popular is that of a pick-pocket pulling your pant leg to get into your trouser pocket and steal your wallet. Well, enough of that. How are you doing, really?"

Nick took a couple slow deep breaths before answering, "I would probably use the term 'bitter-sweet' to describe my time right now. The loss of my family is huge to me, but I know the reality of 'they're not dead' too. I often expect to walk into a room at home and see the kids playing. Stuff like that."

Jonathan reached out a hand across the table, "Take my hand," and he reached out like he was going to arm wrestle. Nick took his hand and leaned into the arm-wrestling position. "We've done this little exercise before, but I want to repeat it for emphasis. I notice you took a deep breath before your last answer. I want you to take three more slow deep breaths."

Nick smiled, "Then crush the back of your hand to the table?"

Jonathan matched his smile, "No, not that,"

Nick took the first breath, then the second, and on the third one something happened inside of him. It was like a shiver, but warm and lasted longer.

Jonathan asked, "What did you just feel?"

Nick's smile had softened, "I think last time we said it was 'hope.'"

Again Jonathan's smile matched Nick's, "Yes, and let it continue to expand and grow in your heart."

Nick took another deep breath as he said slowly, "I will." He reluctantly let go of Jonathan's hand.

Jonathan put his palms flat on the edge of the table as he pushed himself away from it. "I have to go to my next appointment. Thanks for this time, and good job with Freddy. I think that is the beginning of something," and his smile deepened again, "very good."

Nick watched longingly as Jonathan stood up, "And thank you for your time," and he patted his chest, "and more hope."

Jonathan pointed up, "It's His, and He has lots to spare." He turned and walked out the door.

Nick watched out the window as Jonathan walked to the corner where a homeless man sat with his "Anything would help," sign and crouched down to talk to him. He thought to himself, "He never said that he wasn't an angel. Hmmm."

Chapter Twelve: Thursday

Nick sat at his favorite table, at his favorite place, eating his favorite breakfast when Freddy walked up to his table with his own breakfast tray in hand. Nick looked up from the pile of forms he was working through. "Freddy, when did you walk in? I'm sorry, sit down," and he moved aside some of the forms.

Freddy moved his breakfast off the tray and onto the table, "I'll be right back." He took the tray to the top of the automatic waste bin where the used trays were stacked, walked back to the table, and sat. "I think I nearly gave Julie a heart attack when I ordered. Last time I had a gun in my hand."

Nick started to get up, "Do I need to go talk to her?"

Freddy chuckled, "No, no, we had a good laugh about it. I told her that in a rather round-about-way you were paying for my breakfast and I think she had them throw in a couple extra tater tots."

Nick sat back down, "Good, good…and good to see you, too. How are things?"

Freddy got suddenly serious, "Why didn't you tell me that your wife and daughters had just been killed in an auto accident?"

Nick took a slow deep breath, "I was helping you at that point. How did you find out?"

Freddy's smile returned, "I had lunch here yesterday and your friend Jonathan was here. He told me."

Nick sighed, "Well, I guess it wasn't told to him in confidence."

Freddy spoke and his voice was laced with compassion, "To ask if you're doing okay seems trite, but then so does asking if there is anything I can do."

Nick was touched by his concern, but brushed it off with, "Not robbing any other stores would be a good start," and he chuckled under his breath.

"Well," and he sat up a little taller, "I can attest to the fact that I haven't done any of that recently and don't plan on it either." They chuckled there together for a moment and the atmosphere lightened.

Continuing to smile, Nick pulled another business card out of his pocket, "Some good news. My friend Ken owns a lumber yard here in town and is looking for a forklift driver. I gave him your name. He's expecting your call."

Freddy was genuinely surprised, "Really?" Nick nodded and handed him the card. "Do I need to dress up?"

Nick's chuckle returned, "Not to apply for a forklift driver's job."

Freddy's smile matched Nick's, "Yea, I guess not. I'll go see him after breakfast. Do I need to call first?"

"He's expecting a call. So, yes it would be a good idea to do that out of respect for his time. Then you can set up a time to meet with him."

Freddy pointed to the stack of forms, "What's all that?"

"Ah, there is a lot more to someone dying than the hole you leave in the life of those you leave behind. Hence, the forms. Some people even want original copies of the death certificate. I suppose there are those who try to make money faking that people are dead, but even that sounds like a lot of work. Why not just go get a job?" Nick looked at Freddy over the top of his glasses, "Or come talk with me at Chick-fil-A?"

Chapter Thirteen:
The Memorial Service

Nick had taken the next full week off of school in order to make all of the final arrangements. Now, the sanctuary was packed with hardly an empty seat, and it was a large sanctuary. Nick's wife, Ann, was an incredible woman who had helped so many that they probably could have rented the local sports arena and filled it. His daughters too were beloved by many who were attending the service with their parents. Although Nick had asked that donations be made to the "Rescue the Children" foundation in the name of his wife and kids, the front of the sanctuary was still decked out in beautiful floral arrangements surrounding portraits for the three of them.

Nick stepped up to the podium and a hush fell on the audience, "It might seem a little strange, almost macabre that Ann and I had planned out our memorial services years ago, but I don't have to guess at how she would like to be remembered. She wanted us to start with some worship, so if you would stand with me?" Those assembled stood to their feet. Nick then spoke to Jesus as though He was there, because He was. "Jesus, although from our viewpoint their lives were cut short, it was only their time here, standing with us, that has ceased. They are more alive with You than ever." He paused, "And while that loss is difficult for us, their freedom from the shackles of life here is something that we can celebrate. So, we will lift up our hearts and voices in worship to You for Your unspeakable gift of everlasting life. Amen."

There were a chorus of "Amen's" from those attending. Nick backed away from the podium and Victoria walked over to the microphone that stood before the worship band.

She began, "Although our time together this morning is bittersweet, we have the opportunity to worship the One who has given us eternal life. Ann has picked a number of songs to assist us, some old, some new. Shall we begin? Jesus, you have given us life. Life today and life forever. We celebrate both." The music began behind her. "The words, if you need them, are in your bulletin. You may sit, stand, kneel, or whatever aids your worship," and she began to sing:

"The church's one foundation is Jesus Christ her Lord;
She is his new creation By water and the Word.
From heaven he came and sought her To be his holy bride;
With his own blood he bought her, And for her life he died.

Elect from every nation, Yet one o'er all the earth;
Her charter of salvation, One Lord, one faith, one birth;
One holy name she blesses, Partakes one holy food,
And to one hope she presses, With every grace endued.

Mid toil and tribulation, And tumult of her war,
She waits the consummation Of peace forevermore;
Till, with the vision glorious, Her longing eyes are blest,
And the great church victorious Shall be the church at rest.

Yet she on earth hath union With God the Three in One,
And mystic sweet communion With those whose rest is won.
O happy ones and holy! Lord, give us grace that we
Like them, the meek and lowly, On high may dwell with thee."

The next song was a more contemporary one called, I can Only Imagine. When the song finished, a holy hush had enveloped all those who were there, punctuated by some soft weeping. Trying not to disturb the atmosphere, Victoria spoke slightly above a whisper, "You may be seated."

There was a slight rustle as those who had been standing sat. Those kneeling remained so.

Nick had stepped up to the podium again, "A number of years ago I wrote and directed an Easter play called, 'Easter through Heaven's Eyes.' It closed with this song." He stepped back.

Mark had joined Victoria, but with his own microphone. The music began and so did he:

"We knew he was dead 'it is finished,' he said
We had watched as his life ebbed away
(Victoria joined him)
Then we all stood around till the guards took him down
Joseph begged for his body that day

It was late afternoon when we got to the tomb
Wrapped his body and sealed up the grave
So I know how you feel his death was so real
But please listen and hear what I say

(They sang the Chorus together)
I've just seen Jesus I tell you he's alive
I've just seen Jesus our precious Lord alive
And I knew, he really saw me too
As if 'til now, I'd never lived
All that I'd done before won't matter anymore
I've just seen Jesus and I'll never be the same again

(Mark started again)
It was his voice she first heard those kind gentle words
Asking what was her reason for tears

(Victoria took over)
And I sobbed in despair, 'My Lord is not there'
He said, 'Child! it is I, I am here!'

(Chorus together again followed by)
I've just seen Jesus
I've just seen Jesus
All that I'd done before won't matter anymore
I've just seen Jesus and I'll never be the same again
(and the Finale together) *I've just seen Jesus!"*

The holy hush had returned, and pastor Tom stepped up to the podium. "Nick has asked our good friend Kaiser to share a few words with you." Tom stepped back and Kaiser stepped to the podium.

"My friends and friends of Nick, Ann, and the girls, if you have not met Jesus I would plead with you to meet Him today! This is much more than just knowing about Him. This is actually having a relationship with Him. You can believe all the information about Him you want, but you can't have a relationship with information. You can only have a relationship with a living being." He looked around himself, "Can you have a relationship with a tree? Maybe on Vashon Island they think they can. That's where I grew up and Vashon is known for its New Agers and 'Tree Huggers.' You can have some kind of a relationship with your dog or cat, but I am speaking about a relationship with another person, the person of Jesus Christ.

I was sitting at my favorite coffee shop, drinking tea, when a man came up and asked if he could share my table with me. I said, 'Of course,' and before he sat down, I reached out my hand, 'Kaiser.'

He grasped my hand with, 'Ibrahim,' and then he sat. He noticed I was reading and he asked me, 'What are you reading?'

'I'm reading the Bible.' I said.

He pulled out the book that he had under his arm, 'the Qur'an.'

'Ah, you're Muslim?'

'Yes,' he said. 'I teach Arabic at our local Mosque.'

I asked him, 'Do you know Jesus?'

He replied, 'Yes.'

I asked him, 'When did you meet Him?'

He looked somewhat confused, 'What?'

I restated my question, 'When did you meet Jesus?'

He chuckled, 'I haven't met Him,' and he left the sentence trailing.

'Oh,' I continued, 'you know about Jesus. You believe that he is a prophet.'

He countered with a, 'Yes.'

'In the Family of Amran, verse 46,' and I pointed to his Qur'an, 'It identifies Jesus as the Messiah.'

He opened his copy of the Qur'an, turned to the passage, read it for himself, then said, 'Yes.'

'What does it mean, to call him the Messiah? It calls no other prophet the Messiah.' I was smiling slightly and praying silently.

'Messiah means to be anointed or empowered,' Ibrahim responded.

I went on, 'A few verses later it says that Jesus was anointed to heal the blind, cleanse the lepers, even raise the dead. How many prophets do you know who did that?'

He thought for a moment, 'Well, Elijah raised the widow from Zarephath's son from the dead.'

'That's right. Jesus, on the other hand, raised Jairus' daughter, who had just died, from the dead. He also raised the widow at Nain's son, who had been dead long enough that they were on their way to bury him. And Jesus raised Lazarus from the dead, who had been buried for four days and they were worried that when opening the tomb it would release a stench.' Ibrahim was listening intently. I asked, 'Can I tell you a story?' He nodded his assent. I opened my Bible to Mark chapter two and began:

'Jesus was at home teaching and the room was so full of people that there was nowhere to even stand. Four men brought their friend, who was paralyzed and lying on a pallet, to the house, but could not get in because of the crowd. So, they went up on the roof, took apart some of the tiles, tied ropes to the four corners of the pallet, and lowered him to lay at Jesus' feet. Seeing their faith, Jesus said to the man, 'Son, your sins are forgiven.''

I paused for a moment.

'The religious leaders in attendance were incensed, saying, 'This is blasphemy! Who can forgive sins but God alone (it should have been a hint)?' Jesus, perceiving their questioning says, 'Why are you questioning like this? Which is it easier to say to this paralyzed man: that his sins are forgiven or to say to him, Rise up, take up your bed, and walk? But so that you may know that the Son of Man has the authority on earth to forgive sins,' he turned to the paralyzed man and said, 'Rise, pick up your bed, and walk.' And the man rose up, picked up his bed, and walked out before them all. The people were amazed.'

I looked at Ibrahim as I said, 'I don't know of any prophets who forgive sins.'

He sat there dumbfounded. I asked, 'Would you like Him to do that for you, forgive your sins?'

Ibrahim whispered incredulously, 'He can do that?' I simply nodded my head. He asked, 'How?'

I took a deep breath, 'You were designed to be in a relationship with God. You have a spirit, and it has three functions. The first function is called communion. You were designed to be connected to God, but because you have done wrong (sin) you have broken that connection. That wrong is now getting in the way of your having a connection to God.

The second function is intuition. You were designed to get information from God directly. He would speak to you, and you could hear Him. The third function is conscience. This is not the knowing of right from wrong, good from evil. That is fallen conscience and comes from the wrong tree. This is the conscience that Adam had in the beginning. He made his decisions based on the information that he got from his connection with God.'

I took another deep breath and continued, 'If we remove the wrong, you can be reconnected to God and your spirit function in the way it was designed.'

Ibrahim's eyes were wide with surprise as he asked, 'How can I get rid of my wrong?'

I replied, 'Jesus died to take away your wrong and rose from the dead to reconnect you to God.' I did not use the term 'Allah,' but he understood me. 'You just need to ask him to. You can talk to him like he was sitting right there,' and I motioned to the chair next to us, 'because He is here. If I stand behind you, you can't see me, but I am still here. You can talk to me and I to you. It's like that. He is here, you just can't see Him.'

Ibrahim looked down at the table, 'What do I say?'

I put my head lower, towards the table, and he looked up at me, 'Just ask Him to take away your wrong.' I added, 'Out loud.'

Ibrahim took a slow shuddering breath then said just above a whisper, 'Jesus, please take away my wrong.'

I coaxed him some more, 'And ask Him to reconnect you to God.'

He spoke a little stronger, 'and please reconnect me to God.'

I waited a moment and then asked, 'Well?'

A look of amazement slowly graced his face and he said, 'I think He did.' I smiled and reached out my hand. He took it in both of his. There were tears in his eyes, 'That's what being connected to God feels like?'

My spirit said yes, so I nodded. I asked, 'Do you have a Bible?' He shook his head. 'Have you ever read the gospels?' He shook his head again. I opened up my Bible to the book of John, took a business card out of my pocket, and placed it in the Bible. 'Read the first three chapters of John and then call me and we'll get together and chat about what you have found.' We met weekly for quite a while and he led his entire family to Jesus.

"You may think that it sounds simplistic. All I have to do is ask Jesus to take away my wrong and reconnect me to God. Yup, that's the start. I'm not sure why it seems to be so complicated, why we have added all these rules and these ceremonies. Well, that's religion. I am telling you that you can have a relationship with the God of the Universe. I know that this is supposed to be a time of honoring Ann, her daughters, and their lives, but she asked me to settle this first. If you would like to have Jesus take away your wrong, and connect you to God so you can begin a relationship with him today, stand up. Not bow your head, close your eyes, and raise your hand in secret. If you really want to get right with Him right here, right now, stand up."

All over the auditorium people began standing, until there were about fifty people on their feet. Many were weeping softly; most had their heads down.

Kaiser continued, "I want you to come down to the front," and he gestured towards the front of the stage. "Those of you who already have a relationship with Jesus, would you also stand and come down to the front to stand beside one of these who have already come forward?"

Another whole group of people stood and came to the front and stood by those already there. "The service will resume in a few minutes. Please be praying while these folks down here in front take advantage of this opportunity to meet the God of the Universe." Victoria stepped up to the keyboard and began playing softly in the background. This holy moment lasted about five minutes and then people began returning to their seats. There were tears, but now there were mostly smiles and faces filled with hope. Victoria led them in a final worship song and then Kaiser read a combined obituary for Ann and the kids.

Beginning that next week Nick made it a special opportunity to present some very crucial things to the students in his Life Skills class. "There are a number of things we will look at in these next few days that you may not currently see as important. However, from my recent experience I can assure you that they are vital." From behind his desk he brought up a ten by twelve by eight-inch file box and sat it on his desk. He stopped, overcome with emotion. The feeling intensified, tears formed.

Jack stood up, "Mr. Grant, are you okay?"

He held up a hand and took a moment more to regain his composure, took his handkerchief out to wipe his eyes, and took a slow, deep breath. Then he continued, "This may look like a normal file box, but let me assure you that it is not. It is a fireproof, document, storage container. You can purchase one for less than fifty dollars and each of you should have one." He stopped again, another deep breath, "In it you will store all your important papers: your high school diploma, hopefully your college one too. You will also want it to contain your birth certificate, passport, the title to your car and house, when you get one. It's a good place to also store your insurance policies and everything else that you deem important like: a list of banks, accounts, credit cards and any financial institutions where you have money." He took still another deep breath, "You need the original of your will and any other documents regarding the disposition of your assets when you take the ultimate upgrade."

That got a few chuckles, "You mean when you die?" came from the back class.

"Yes! I know right now you feel immortal, but you're not, and it pays to be prepared, especially for those you leave behind." He paused again, "Get in groups of three or four and brainstorm a list of what other important things you might want in your box."

Just before the bell rang Nick concluded with, "We'll start class tomorrow sharing our lists of important things. If you are interested in getting yourself a box, I have worked a deal with BigBuy. I have coupons up here at my desk that will get you a discount on a box when you tell them you are from my class. Come up and get one if you want." The bell rang and a number of students filed up to Nick's desk to get a coupon.

Chapter Fourteen:
You Want Me to go Where?

A few weeks had passed since the memorial service for Ann and the girls. Nick was sitting in the living room drinking an ice-cold Cherry Coke when he felt a rather unmistakable prompting, "Go to Terry's Tavern, just down the street." He had never been there, and it felt a little strange, but the urge to go seemed difficult to withstand. So, he went. It was a little after 6 pm and was not very crowded. Most people were probably at home having their supper. Nick approached the bartender, who asked, "What can I get for you?"

Nick responded hesitantly, "You wouldn't have Cherry Coke, would you?"

The bartender smiled, "It's your lucky day, I do."

Nick returned his smile, "Cold, but no ice, please."

The bartender set the glass down in front of Nick, "My name is Terry, like the tavern." He chuckled, "You're new here?"

Sheepishly Nick replied, "Yup, first time, I'm Nick," and held out his hand.

Terry grasped his hand firmly, "Then the first one's on me."

Nick was pleasantly surprised, "Why, thank you."

And he was even more surprised when Terry said, "As they say at Chick-fil-A, 'My pleasure.'" Suddenly, Nick knew he was in the right place. Terry pointed towards the back, "There are pool tables in the back, a buck a rack."

"Thanks," Nick picked up his drink, it was frosty cold, and headed for the back room.

The room was well lit, included three pool tables and an assortment of chairs. He set his drink down on a side table, grabbed a rack off the wall, and found a bill reader at the end of the pool table. He took out a dollar bill, fed it into the reader, and the balls dropped into the receptacle. He racked up the balls, rehung the rack on the wall, selected a cue stick, grabbed some chalk, and chalked his cue as he walked to the other end of the table with the cue ball.

He thought to himself, *"Why am I here?"* Well, it was probably more of a question to God. He took a deep breath, lined up the cue ball to the racked balls, and smoothly stroked the ball. It had been forever since he had played pool. They had a table at home that doubled as a ping pong table and he had played a little in college, but nothing since then. There was a resounding "crack", and the balls scattered all over. He saw one of the solids drop in the corner pocket. *"I guess we start with solids."* He thought. He had finished the solids and was starting on the stripes when he noticed a guy standing, leaning against the door jam.

Nick nodded to him, and he nodded back. He ran the rest of the table.

The guy stepped forward, his hand outstretched, "My friends call me Jimmy." Nick grabbed his hand firmly. "Fancy a game? But not for money after that demonstration."

Nick grinned, "Nick, sure, just a friendly game."

Jimmy fed a dollar into the reader and the balls dropped, as Nick retrieved the rack from the wall. Jimmy loaded it, positioned the balls, and placed the rack back on the wall. "Do you mind if I go first so I at least get a chance to play?" and he snickered.

"It's your dollar, Jimmy."

It was then that Nick noticed a cue case on the table next to the door. Jimmy went over, opened the case, assembled his cue stick, selected a chalk, and walked to the other end of the table with the cue ball in hand.

Nick shook his head, "Tell me that wasn't a bit intimidating, Jimmy?"

Jimmy winked, lined himself up, and stroked the cue ball. Another resounding "crack" echoed as the balls scattered. A stripe dropped in the side pocket, "Guess I'm stripes." He was quite good. After the second game, they had each won one, Nick excused himself to replenish his drink, "Do you want anything from the bar?"

"A beer would be nice? Fancy another game?"

"Yes, any particular brand of beer?" Nick added.

Jimmy winked again, "Terry knows me."

Nick walked to the bar and Terry met him, "How much did he take you for?"

Nick chortled, "I think he's still getting my measure. We're one a piece."

Terry was impressed, "Whoa, you must be pretty decent yourself then."

"It has been a while," Nick admitted. "Another Cherry Coke for me and a beer for Jimmy."

"Would you like to start a tab?" Terry asked politely.

"I must look trustworthy, sure." Nick joked.

"If you can beat Jimmy, I'm sure that you're good for your drinks," Terry nodded.

"Is Jimmy a regular?" Nick tried not to sound too inquisitive.

"Yup, and State pool champ the last three years running," Terry retorted.

"I was a little intimidated with the pool case," Nick admitted.

"It was a gift from a friend back when he was a lot younger," Terry confided.

Nick carefully grabbed the two drinks and headed back to the pool room. "Thanks."

Jimmy had racked the balls and was waiting for him. There was a gal there now too. "Nick, this is Janet. She'd like to watch us play if you don't mind." She had her own drink in her hand. She seemed about Jimmy's age, nicely dressed in slacks and a light blue blouse. A jacket matching the slacks hung over the chair she stood by.

Nick approached her, hand outstretched, and repeated his name, "Nick, I hope he finds your presence intimidating," and grinned.

She met his gaze directly and took his hand, "Nothing much intimidates Jimmy regarding pool, sorry." Her light laugh reminded him of something. Ann, she reminded him of Ann.

"Darn!" was all Nick could say.

They hadn't spoken much during their first two games. Jimmy must have felt more comfortable now that Janet was there. "So Nick, what do you do for a living?" A typical guy question.

"I teach psychology and life sciences at the high school." It was Nick's turn to break.

"Have you figured me out already?" Jimmy asked, jokingly.

Nick shook his head, "Not during our first encounter. It takes longer than that for me. What do you do?"

"Well, Janet thinks I should play pool professionally, but that would take all the fun out of it. I'm actually a dealer at the casino when I'm not here at Terry's." He laid his cue stick on the table, reached in his back pocket, and pulled out a deck of cards. He opened the deck, took out the cards, and laid the pack on the table. He expertly shuffled the cards, ending with a fan to them, then said, "Pick a card, any card."

Nick's eyes widened, "You're a magician too?" He picked a card, looked at it, and handed it back to him, placing it in the middle of the fanned deck.

Jimmy shuffled again and handed the deck to Nick. "Cut the deck and turn over the cut." Nick did just that. "Is that your card?" It was.

"How on earth did you do that?" Nick was in awe.

Jimmy just laughed and sunk the next ball.

After that evening, Nick came to Terry's Tavern a couple nights a week and often played pool with Jimmy. This evening the other two tables were filled as well, and things were pretty raucous. Nick looked over to the doorway after he sunk his ball. The lights from the other room were blocked out by a huge guy who took up most of the doorway.

The huge man walked over to Nick and Jimmy's table and started pushing and pulling balls into the pockets with a, "This is my table, you guys are done."

Jimmy was about to take a swing at him with his custom cue stick when Nick stepped in front of him, "We were in the middle of a game," Nick said to the man's back, "You owe us a dollar." The huge bear of a man pivoted quickly around.

"I said you're done. So, you're done," he growled.

"No!" Nick heard an unmistakable, "Fold your hands" in his head. He did. The bear took a swing at Nick, and it was like his hand hit an invisible wall. He brought back his hand shaking it, looking at it like it obviously hurt. He growled and made as if to charge but found that he could not move.

Nick spoke quite calmly, "Your name, sir?"

The bear shook his head like someone was inside his head rattling around. He spoke slowly, "Napoleon, but they call me 'Pole.'"

Nick held out his hand, "You owe me a dollar." Pole took out his wallet, removed a dollar, and held it out to Nick. Nick took the dollar, "Pole, you may leave and not return this evening."

Pole looked down at his empty hand, put his wallet back in his pocket, turned, and walked back out through the door. Jimmy just stood there with his mouth open as Nick inserted the bill into the bill reader and the balls dropped.

"I guess we have to start that game over again. Whose turn is it to break?"

Jimmy just pointed at him while all those at the other tables stood there dumbfounded.

The next evening was similarly crowded. Nick and Jimmy were playing, and the other tables were full. This time Pole entered with two of his buddies. They were not as large as Pole, but still seemed formidable. Nick hesitated only a moment before throwing his pool cue to Jimmy and grabbing another off the wall. Jimmy put his stick down on the table as he caught the cue that Nick threw. Together they faced the three brutes with pool cues they were prepared to swing like baseball bats. They broke their cues across the two smaller brutes who went down like felled trees. Having completed their arcs they were prepared to address Pole together, but Pole caught a cue in each hand and disarmed them. He dropped the cues to the ground and stood to face Jimmy. His fist caught him on the chin and lifted him totally off the ground to land like a discarded rag doll at his feet. Pole then turned to face Nick. Nick folded his hands like the night before, but Pole stepped forward, grabbed Nick by the throat and lifted him off the ground. The last thing Nick saw was the monster grinning, then only blackness.

Chapter Fifteen:
The Hospital

His eyelids fluttered open and while the subdued lights of the hospital room were dimmed, they still seemed very bright compared to the darkness he had been experiencing. Someone held his hand. Nick slowly opened his eyes again, just a slit. It was Muriel. He hadn't seen her in years. Perhaps it was just a dream. He blinked again as he heard her say, "Nick? Are you awake?"

Nick smiled, "Is this heaven?"

"No, silly. You're in a hospital. You were in a fight in a bar. What were you doing in a bar?" She seemed quite surprised.

Nick tried to think back, but nothing came to him, "You must be mistaken. I don't remember any of that."

"Well, you have been in a coma, so I wouldn't be too surprised at some partial amnesia for a time," she responded casually.

Perplexed, he inquired, "How did you come to find me?"

She smiled. He remembered that smile. "I work at admitting here and saw your name pop up on the roster of new arrivals."

He went to put his other hand on hers too, but did so carefully. There was an IV in a vein on the back of it. "How long was I out?"

"This is the third day. They didn't know how long you had been oxygen deprived when the aid cars arrived. They were starting to worry. It seems it was you and a fellow named Jimmy against three brutes. You took care of two of them, but the largest one knocked Jimmy unconscious and was choking you to death when a bystander broke a chair over his head."

Expressing some concern, "And the others?"

"Oh, they have all been released. There is an officer here to talk with you. Let me go tell them all that you are awake." She reluctantly released his hand. "I have to go to work, but I'll drop in on you again after my shift." She was gone before he could respond. He was still a little befuddled.

A nurse came in followed by a police officer, "Nick, how do you feel?" She seemed somehow familiar.

"Okay, I think. You tell me." He smiled weakly.

She took his vital signs, "Hmm, that's better. Are you up to answering a few questions from this officer?"

Nick looked to the officer, "I think so."

The officer sighed, "What do you remember about how you got here in the hospital?"

Nick paused, thinking back. It was starting to return to him. "A huge man named Pole and two of his friends attacked Jimmy and I at Terry's Tavern back in the pool room."

"Yes, that's the consensus of those I've talked to. I need to know if you want to press assault charges against them?" That seemed pretty simple to the officer.

"What did Jimmy say?"

The officer sighed again, "He said that it was up to you, assuming you regained consciousness. If you didn't, I should come to talk to him again."

"Do you need to know right away or can I think about it?" Nick queried.

"There's no hurry, with Pole's size he's not very difficult to find." The officer turned and left the room.

The nurse returned, "Can I get you anything for pain or anything at all?"

Nick lifted his hand, "Do I still need this thing?"

She had dimples when she smiled it suddenly reminded him of Ann and he felt again the sharp pain of her loss, "I'll give the doctor a call and he will be in later this evening to talk to you."

"Thanks, okay if I take a nap?" She checked his pupils again and their response to light and pronounced a nap a good idea. He closed his eyes and was out before she left the room.

He stepped right into the middle of a dream. He was Tevye, performing in Fiddler on the Roof with his community theater. He was standing next to Muriel singing, "Do you love me?" and her response, "Do I what?" The crowd cheered as they finished the song.

He drifted towards wakefulness, remembering that moment. It was the highlight of his short acting career. He had done it on a lark and Ann had put up with all the rehearsals and his singing the songs around the house for months. Muriel had played his wife, and she was incredible. It was the first time she had been in a lead role, but they just hit it off. The short run of the production had been to rave reviews. They had never again collaborated as closely but remained friends and been in a few other productions together. He didn't realize that she had moved to hospital admissions. He had to admit that he had enjoyed waking up to see her and it was nice to have someone there. He drifted off again.

This time he awoke again as someone had taken his hand. It was Muriel, "Hi, big guy. How's your memory now?"

He squeezed her hand, "Just fine thanks and thanks for stopping by." He looked at his other hand and realized the IV was gone, its only evidence a Band-Aid.

She wrinkled up her nose, "As they say at Chick-fil-A, 'My pleasure.' Your doctor is making rounds and should be here shortly. I should probably go."

Nick held on as if for dear life, "Please don't. Can you stay for just a bit?"

She gave a mock sigh, "Oh, I guess I could for a bit." She paused, "I'm sorry I missed the funeral." Then she looked away, "Did you know that my husband died recently too?"

He squeezed her hand, "No, I didn't. I'm sorry."

She took a deep breath, "It was probably for the best. He had cancer and they didn't give him long. It was quick and virtually painless, a blessing really."

Still squeezing her hand, "Still, I know it's difficult even when somewhat expected."

She looked back into his eyes, "At least no children to miss him, but then none to comfort me either."

The moment was shattered by a knock on his hospital room door and the doctor stepped into the room. Muriel offered, "I'll leave you two alone."

To which Nick countered, "No need, you can stay," so she just got up and moved her chair back from the bed.

The doctor stepped forward, his hand extended, "Dr. Owens. How's my patient?"

Nick sat up as he shook the doctor's hand, "Great! What do I need to do to blow this popsicle stand?"

The doctor looked at his chart, "Have you had anything to eat?"

"No, I haven't," and he suddenly realized that he was hungry. Just then his nurse popped in.

The doctor looked at her, "Nurse, get this man some food and if he can keep it down then he's free to go home."

As the doctor turned back to Nick she gave him a mock salute, "Yes, sir," turned and left to get him some food.

"There were initially some problems with your memory. That's pretty normal. How's it now?" He didn't seem all that concerned.

"It seems fine, Dr. Owens," addressing him by his name to show both that he had heard it and had remembered it.

"Fine, I'm glad you're doing okay. We were a bit concerned, but I'll go fill out your release, assuming you keep your supper down." The doctor pivoted and left the room.

"Thanks," Nick called out after him.

Muriel still stood there, "Would you like me to wait and take you home?"

Nick sighed, "Yes, just give me a minute to change out of this cute, backless gown and then if my supper stays down we will be on our way."

She turned and left his room, with a quick smile.

He was in his clothes by the time the nurse returned with his supper, macaroni and cheese and a cream of vegetable soup. He called Muriel back into his room and ate as fast as he could. He then had Muriel go ask the nurse how long they needed to wait to assure that he could keep it down. She suggested a half an hour and returned in twenty minutes with the paperwork he needed to sign to be released. It was company policy to take him downstairs in a wheel chair, so he got a little ride to the front door of the hospital where Muriel waited with her car. When they got to his place, she walked him to his door, gave him a hug and turned to leave.

"Can I take you out to dinner tomorrow night?" he asked.

She turned back to face him, "Yes, I'd like that. I have tomorrow off."

"Would six o'clock be too early?" He looked hopeful.

She smiled, "That will be fine. I'll see you then."

"Thanks again for everything,"

And she replied with, "As they say at Chick-fil-A..."

"I know, I know, it was your pleasure," and he watched her walk back to her car, get in, and leave.

Chapter Sixteen:
Dinner with Muriel

Nick awoke in the safety and security of his own bed, among all the old familiar sounds and smells. He looked over to see Ann sleeping beside him. He was shocked. He blinked and she vanished to be replaced by the dark pain of loss. This, however, was a new day, could he face it with anticipation? He hoped that he could. He stood beneath the deluge of a hot shower for a long time. He could stand there as long as he wanted. There was no one else to use up all the water in the hot water heater.

He quickly toweled off, noticed the Band-Aid remnants of his IV, peeled the wet thing off his hand, and discarded it in the trash. He dressed in the clothes he had laid out before falling asleep, but almost forgot to tie his shoes in his haste to get to Chick-fil-A before it opened. After lacing them up, he grabbed his Bible, notebook, and took out his keys to lock the door behind himself. He stopped for a moment on the back porch and breathed deeply in the fragrances of Ann's handiwork. It was a beautifully landscaped backyard. He could hear the light tinkling of the fountain in the pond. Hmm, the coons had left it alone last night. That was a good sign.

Chick-fil-A was only a little over a mile from his home. He could have walked, but then he would have had to walk back on a full stomach. Maybe he would walk later. He got there just as Ed walked out the front door and waved to him on his way to

open the drive-thru. His Cherry Coke awaited him at his table. He called it his office and last spring, Ranae, the owner, had installed a brass plaque on the wall to that effect. It read:
"Mr. Nick's Office
Regular hours Mon-Sat 6:30-7:30am
Other times by appointment only."

He ordered on the App, but Julie brought it almost before he was done. She uncharacteristically sat at his table. "Are you alright? We heard about the fight at Terry's Tavern. We have all been praying for you."

It almost brought tears to his eyes, "Yes, I'm fine." Then he laughed, "You should see the other guy. Thanks for your prayers."

She reached over and put her hand on the back of his, "Our pleasure." She squeezed his hand and got up. Nick winked, opened his ranch sauce, tater tots, and Bible, breathed a short sigh, said, "Thanks," and started eating and reading. He was in Proverbs, chapter three,

"Do not forget my teaching, but let your heart keep my commandments, for length of days and years of life and peace they will add to you."

It always seemed so simple, not easy, but simple. Listen, receive, respond, and do.

Saturday was laundry and house cleaning day. He didn't have much laundry this week, having been in the hospital, and the house should be relatively clean for the same reason. He decided to do the laundry anyway. He plugged in the electric tea pot, dropped the door for the laundry chute, sorted the lights and darks, and got the first load going. He could probably do the laundry only every other week now that Ann and the kids were gone, except that he'd run out of underwear. He laughed to himself, "Who needs to wear underwear?" He remembered when he had been student teaching so many years ago. He and another teacher were helping coach basketball after school. As they changed into shorts and t-shirts he noticed the other guy didn't wear any undershorts. As Nick stood there with his mouth open, the guy smiled, "Military. You often didn't have time to put on your shorts. After a while you quit trying."

He made a quick cup of decaf and took it to his home office. He took out his lesson plan notebook. He'd missed a couple of days with his hospitalization, but if they had gotten Mr. Gunderson to substitute for him again then he knew he would still be up to date. That kid was incredible, and the students loved him.

Shortly after ten, he went out to the garage, got some dog biscuits, and went over to visit the neighbor's dog. He had been doing this for years. He was Stacy's dog-father. His neighbors let him come over and play with her whenever he liked and he tried to get over there daily, but more on weekends. She greeted him at the fence, leaping up and down as he approached. She was pretty old, but always perked up when he came over. He broke the biscuits in half, they were easier to eat that way. Then they just hugged for a bit. No playing fetch today.

On the way back to his place he noticed the grass could use a cut. It was still a bit wet from the sprinklers, but he would put that on his list for the afternoon. Back in the house, he put the first load in the dryer, the second in the washer, and went back to his office.

He was working on a novel, his third. He was experiencing a tad bit of writer's block. He went back and reread the last chapter till he got to where he was,

> "She stood with the horses. They were still traveling during the night and sleeping during the day. They had made camp and she was taking care of the horses while the others started the fire for supper."

That's where he was stuck. He prayed and waited.

"She had her hand on the neck of the bay when it whinnied. There was a response from a horse nearby, not one of theirs. She turned to face the threat as she heard a sword clear its sheath and a note of the purest joy. There in the morning light stood a man, sword in hand."

Nick thought to himself, *"What? Who is this?"* Well, at least he had broken through the writer's block. The story slowly unfolded for the next hour and then he went downstairs to take the load out of the dryer, put the other one in the dryer, and then fold the first load. He brought it up and put it away before he went back to his novel. It seemed that his travelers had come across a soldier of fortune who possessed one of the singing swords. Hmmm, how did he come by that? He pondered that for a while until it was time for the next load to come out of the dryer. He folded it and put it away. Time for lunch. He made himself a sandwich, drank some juice, and went out to cut the grass.

That was different too, now that Ann was gone. When she was still there he didn't usually get a chance to cut the grass. That was because he cut the grass in about half an hour. While she manicured the lawn and it normally took about two hours. He stood there with his hands on the lawn mower, the garage door open. *"Cut the grass, or manicure the lawn? Cut the grass or manicure the lawn?"* He decided to just cut the grass. After he was done, in about thirty minutes, he went back to his office. He had just sat down when his computer dinged with a new notification. It was an email from Muriel, "Looking forward to tonight, here's my address. See you at six."

He smiled shyly, he was looking forward to meeting her tonight too. He sent back, "Me 2, C U at 6."

He arrived just before six in slacks, shirt, and tie, but not a suit coat. He rang the bell, and she opened the door. Some might have thought Muriel plain, but hers was a natural beauty that didn't need a lot of artificial enhancement.

She smiled broadly, "Hello, let me grab my coat and purse."

He was dumb-founded. He remembered asking himself once, *"What is beauty?"* The answer came back, *"You will know it when you see it."* Yes! In her own way Muriel displayed beauty. He offered her his arm which she took as they walked to the car. He opened her door and closed it once she got in.

"Where would you like to go for dinner?" He inquired and waited.

She looked down at her hands, "Would you feel good or bad if I said Chick-fil-A?"

His eyes widened, "You're kidding?"

She looked back up, "No, a serious question."

"My people and my place?" he exclaimed, "That would be wonderful!"

"Then off we go," and she looked out the car's front windshield. "How was your Saturday?"

He grinned, "Not too bad, I did the laundry, cut the grass. Oh, and I broke out of my writer's block on my story."

"You're writing a story?" She was surprised. She hadn't realized he was a writer too.

"Yup, my third novel. The first one took twenty-five years, the second one less than sixty days, and I hope to publish the third one this year." He was rightfully proud.

"What are they about?" It was a logical question.

The first two are apocalyptic and this one started out as a Christmas musical, but has turned into another novel. It kept getting bigger and bigger. Either that or it would have been an epic opera," and he laughed.

"Wow, teaching full time, when have you found time to write?" She seemed intrigued.

"It took about two or three years to get my lesson plans all developed and the girls out of diapers. Then, once they were down for the evening, Ann and I would chat for a bit, and then

I was off to my home office to bang away on the computer for an hour or so." It seemed pretty straight-forward.

"And the Christmas one?" She still sounded interested.

"It's about the Magi and their travels to find the new king of the Jews. It should be fun because most people already know a little of the story. I hope to provide a new and unique perspective."

"Without giving away any spoilers, give me an example," she asked politely.

"Well, one of the reasons that I like to write is because it makes me think of things I have never thought about before. For instance, they are going to find Jesus when he is about two years old. We know this because Herod tries to kill all the children two and under based on when the Magi said they first saw the star. So, what is Jesus like as a two-year old?" Nick asked enthusiastically.

"You're right. I have never thought about that before," she responded.

"And that's just one interesting thing," Nick puffed out his chest.

"When will you be done with it? I'd like to read it." She still appeared sincere.

"I hope to publish it before Christmas, since it's about Christmas. I could give you an early PDF version if you'd like. I'm going to be forming a launch team this time to read it before it's published and then, during the first week it's available, purchase the Kindle version, and review it on Amazon. To sell well on Amazon you need to have a catchy title, an arresting cover, a good 'blurb' explaining the book, and 7-10 good reviews. Let me know if you're interested." Nick was getting more excited himself just explaining all this.

"I'm already interested. What about the first two books?" They were both like two kids with a new toy.

"They are a little complicated, good, but more difficult to follow. I'd start with the Christmas one and see if you like my style." He was trying to underplay how he felt about how enthused she was.

"Okay, if you say so, but the first two are available on Amazon?" It sounded like she might buy them anyway.

"Yup, under my name."

They arrived at Chick-fil-A. It was busy, dinner usually was, but both his parking spot and table were available. A number of the employees greeted him by name, "Heh, Mr. Nick. This is a little late for breakfast. Who's your friend?"

"This is Muriel, she played my wife in *Fiddler on the Roof*." He was tempted to start singing *Do You Love Me?* but didn't want to embarrass her any more than she already was. She sat across the table from him. He had a Chicken Deluxe meal because it was dinner, no lettuce on his sandwich though. She had a Chicken Deluxe meal too, but with the lettuce. He even talked her into fries and a Cherry Coke, but hers included light ice.

Even amidst a crowd of others eating in the restaurant they seemed alone. One of the CFA servers had stopped, taken their empty cups, and returned with their drinks replenished. They were laughing, and simply having a nice time, when Muriel got suddenly silent, looked down at the table, and whispered, "I have cancer." It seemed that everything stopped, and the cacophony of sounds and voices moved to the background.

Nick reached out and took her hand, "How long have you known?"

She smiled weakly, "Not long."

"The prognosis?" It seemed such a simple question.

"I don't have very long, but I am in no pain." She slowly raised her gaze to meet his eyes.

He had to ask and felt the liberty to do so, "And you know Jesus?"

She nodded yes but he needed to clarify. "When did you meet Him?"

Her smile grew, "It's funny that you should ask. It was during Fiddler on the Roof, playing your wife. It was obvious that you were not just playing a role. You really knew God. So, one night I asked our fellow actor, Les, about Him and she introduced me to Him."

Nick sighed deeply and asked for permission from God, which He granted, "That's wonderful. Do you believe that He could heal you right now?"

She smiled, "What about your horse that pulls your milk cart?" referring to a scene from Fiddler on the Roof where Tevye asked God, "Why don't You heal my horse?" And decided that just because God could heal didn't necessarily mean He would.

Nick laughed quietly, "Yes, something like that."

She laughed too at their secret little joke and reached out her other hand.

He now held both her hands as he silently inquired, *"How?"* Then continued, "We, as western American Christians, have a lot of funny ideas. We think everything needs to be a big deal, but it really should be rather simple. Jesus healed a blind man by spitting on the ground, making clay which he put in his eyes, and telling him to go wash out the clay."

Muriel was nodding, there were tears in her eyes. "If I asked you to do something silly, would you?"

She nodded, *"Yes."*

Nick spoke just above a whisper, "Lean forward."

She did.

"I'm going to kiss the back of your hand and you are going to take a slow deep breath. Then I will kiss the other, and you take another slow deep breath."

She whispered back coyly, "You just want to kiss my hands," and giggled.

Nick shook his head, trying to be serious.

She furrowed her brows, "Okay, I'm ready."

He brought one hand to his lips and lightly kissed the back of it. She took her slow deep breath, looking him straight in the eyes. He lifted her other hand and for some reason turned it over and kissed her palm. That surprised her, but what surprised her more was the shiver of warmth that coursed through her entire body as she took the second deep breath. It was delightful and lasted longer than a normal shiver, being repeated three times. Each time it was stronger and longer and her eyes continued to widen. Nick felt it too, like fire coursing through his veins.

He spoke softly, "That was interesting. Did you feel that?"

"Yes," she confessed, "like three surges of warmth, pulsating through my entire body." She hung out her lower lip, "Does that mean you're going to let go of my hands?"

He squeezed them and let go, "Yes it does." He shook his head again, "When is your next doctor's appointment?"

"This next Friday."

He winked at her, "Well, it should confirm what you and I already know."

Muriel folded her hands, sighed, and said warmly, "Thanks, Tevye."

Nick sang softly, "Do you love me?"

She replied, "You're a fool," and they both laughed.

Nick picked up their trays as he got to his feet. As he walked by her, she also got up, took his arm, and they walked to the trash machine. The machine was temperamental but seemed to be working tonight. He touched the door with the tray, the door opened, and he dumped the wrappings from their supper into the box. He set the tray on its top, rearranged the rest of the trays, and she retook his arm. He turned to the counter and waved, receiving a chorus of, "Have a nice evening, Mr. Nick."

He replied, "You too."

Outside, he held her car door open again for her and closed it when she got in.

When they got her home, he walked her to her door.

She turned to him, having unlocked it, "We should do this again. Thanks for everything."

"Sure, where are you going to church tomorrow? Would you like to join me for the early service?" He was not applying pressure. It was just an offer.

She thought a moment, "That would be splendid. Are slacks okay?"

He smiled, "Slacks are fine. I'll swing by about 8:30."

She smiled back, "I'll try to be ready. Thanks again."

It was his turn, "My pleasure." She shook her head as she closed the door.

He headed back to his car, got in his car, and prayed during the trip home.

Chapter Seventeen:
The Next Sunday's Service

He arrived at 8:30 wearing a suit and tie that complimented Muriel's pants, blouse, and sweater. Service started at 9:00, so they had time for coffee and for him to introduce her to a number of raised eyebrows. It was probably his, "This is Muriel, my wife from Fiddler on the Roof" that did it. They sat down front and center. He, Ann, and the kids always had too.

Muriel had a nice voice, although she would deny it. She tended to be self-deprecating. He was pleased when she took a small notebook out of her purse and took notes on Tom's message which always was simple, direct, funny, and to-the-point.

Tom said, "A country pastor was driving past a beautiful plot of land. The rows were plowed long and straight. There wasn't a weed to be seen and the wheat was coming up, looking healthy. The pastor pulled into the driveway to find the farmer working on his tractor. The pastor said, 'That's quite a field. I must say that the Lord has been good to you.'

The farmer replied, 'Thank you, you should have seen it when He had it all to Himself.'"

The congregation laughed politely. It was church after all.

Tom then told the story of a friend of his who he considered to be his challenge in giving. He called him Fred.

Fred told Tom that another mutual friend had once asked him, "You know those guys we hear about who give away ninety percent of their income and live on only the ten percent? How did they get that way?"

Fred said that he had never thought about it. His other friend had said, "Don't you suppose they are just regular guys like you and I?"

"Well," Fred had said, "They probably put their pants on one leg at a time."

His friend continued, "Don't you suppose they just started with the tithe, like you and I, and one year God said, 'I bet you can give twelve percent' and they did, and then He said 'fifteen percent,' and they did. Twenty percent, thirty, until they found that they were there?"

Fred said, "I had never thought of it like that." Fred decided to make it a life goal to give away as much as he was able.

Tom said, "A few years ago I was talking to Fred and he said, "I ran the numbers."

"What?" I asked him, "What numbers?"

"My last year's giving numbers," Fred said. "I found that my tax-deductible charitable giving equaled seventy percent of my income."

Wow," Tom said, "you're almost there."

Fred continued, "I'm not done. My non-tax deductible giving equaled the rest."

"Huh," Tom replied, "the rest?"

"Yup," Fred said, "I gave it all away."

"What? You gave away your entire income? What did you live on, your savings?"

Fred said, "That's the interesting part. I track my net worth and it's better than ever."

"How is that even possible?" Tom asked.

Fred just pointed upward.

Tom continued his message saying, "If your giving is an indicator of how grateful you are for all that God has done for you, are you only ten percent grateful? No! Only one man in scripture was told to give it all away and sadly he did not. But a simple widow gave away all that she had to live on. So what did she live on? God's blessing and provision. How grateful are you for all that He has done for you? How much should you give away to represent that gratefulness, ten percent as Abram did in the beginning, or everything as my friend Fred did? It might be something you'd like to talk to Him about."

Then Tom had everyone stand, sing a song, and recite the Lord's prayer.

It was still a beautiful morning as they walked to the car.

"May I take you to lunch?"

She chuckled under her breath, "It's a little early for lunch, but yes."

He interjected, "How about a drive first?"

"Certainly."

Nick drove to the bluff overlooking the bay. This is where the kids would come and park. They weren't doing that kind of parking, just enjoying the day and each other. Nick brought it up, "How are you feeling after our dinner last night at Chick-fil-A?"

She sat back and sighed deeply, "I haven't felt this good in a long time."

He reached over, offering his hand. She took it, squeezed, and let it go.

"I'm so glad. You know, I'm thinking of retiring from teaching."

She looked at him a little shocked, "I thought you loved teaching?"

It was his turn to sigh, "I do, but I have got a lot I want to do."

There was some concern written on her face, "And for money?"

He chuckled slightly, "I'm doing very well in that aspect. We have always been careful, frugal, and invested wisely. Money won't be a problem."

"What does He think about it?" She pointed up.

He smiled, "I think it was His idea, but we've just started talking about it."

Her concern lessened, "What is it that you want to do?"

"Not travel, if you are worried that I'm going to run off in the middle of some mid-life crisis. I want to simplify. It will take a lot to get the house ready to sell."

"You're going to sell your house? Where will you live?" The concern was coloring her voice again.

"Ah, you don't know that story. I will only move about fifty feet. I own the house next to me. The old gal that lived there got sideways financially and quit paying her mortgage for a couple years. One day a realtor showed up on her doorstep to announce, 'Your house goes on the auction block tomorrow. I think I can get it for one dollar over opening bid cause we all work together at the auction. Do you know anyone that can buy it and rent it back to you?' Long story short, I bought it the next day and began renting it to her really inexpensively. She lived in it until just recently. That's part of what started all this. So, I can move over there, get my house ready and sell it."

"Wouldn't it be easier to sell the house next door?" she offered.

"Yes, but my house is too big and the yard, while beautiful, will be much more than I want to take care of long term. This would be a great time to sell my place while everything is still in great shape." Nick had obviously been thinking about this.

"I thought it was not a good idea to make a lot of life-changing decisions right after someone's passing." She had a point.

"That's true and why we," and he pointed up and then to her, "are having this chat."

She smiled weakly, "Thanks for including me?"

Nick winked, "You're welcome. You want to hear some more?"

She cringed jokingly, "Okay."

"You've never been in my house, but there are a ton of books, I mean a ton. There are like three floor-to-ceiling walls of them. I want to ask Tom if I can set up a library at church. That way I can still check them out if I need them, but don't have to store them."

Muriel cocked her head to the side, "Hmm, who will take care of the library at church?"

"I'm pretty sure someone will step up. It will be a great small commitment way to serve the congregation."

"You've run a church library before?" She wasn't convinced.

"Actually I have, with Ann. Once it's set up, it's not too difficult, just a couple hours a week and a little time Sunday morning." He'd been thinking about that too. "Then there's finishing my Christmas novel and there's a nagging God-thought about its sequel."

She looked down at her hands in her lap, "And you could give up teaching?"

He grinned a little, "There is a great kid who they have substitute when I'm gone or unconscious." He chuckled. "He would be a perfect full-time teacher there at the high school. He already knows my lesson plans, which I would give him, so he would have a two-year head start on teaching my subjects by himself. It would be a lot easier modifying my plans than coming up with them himself."

"And you wouldn't miss that?" Concern returned.

"You know, I've always thought I was a teacher, but what I recently discovered is that I am a 'story-teller,' and sometimes teaching is my venue to tell a story. I would still be a 'story-teller,' just not every day at the high school. It actually feels quite liberating."

"So, I'm just a sounding board for these decisions you've already made?" She was being lightly sarcastic.

He reached over and took her hand again, "No, you are much more than just a 'sounding board,' although by this time you might be getting 'bored.'" He laughed at the pun as he put air quotes around bored. Then he changed the subject. "Where would you like to go for lunch? Chick-fil-A isn't open on Sundays," and he laughed.

"My needs, desires, and wishes are pretty simple. What would you suggest?"

"Well…." He drew out the word. "Sundays should be special. How about Olive Garden?" Before she could answer, he continued, "Actually every day should be special in my book. Romans fourteen says there are two types of Christians. I'm sure there are many types, but these two are: those who esteem one day better than another, and those who esteem all days alike. I am of the latter. I think each and every day should be special." He paused, "Now, what about Olive Garden?"

She just shook her head back and forth, "Okay, on this special day, Olive Garden would be fine."

He turned on the car and they left the bluff for Olive Garden.

After a wonderful lunch, he took her home and walked her again to her door. "Can I call you?"

"Or text or email me, yes. Thanks for a nice morning." She backed into her doorway.

He bowed slightly, "My pleasure."

She shook her head, waved good bye and closed the door. As he walked back to his car she leaned her back against the door, "I wonder where this is going?"

Chapter Eighteen:
Not Just Another Monday

During lunch on Monday he broke the news to his principal. "At the end of the quarter I'm going to retire. You might want to see if you can get Mr. Gunderson full time."

His principal, Hugh Benson, was stunned. He came back with, "This is just a play for more money, right?"

Nick shook his head as he laughed, "No, I'm serious. It's time for the next chapter. Which reminds me, you should have the English Lit classes read my first two books."

Now Mr. Benson shook his own head, "Get out of my office, you scoundrel." He paused. "I'll give Gunderson a call and see if I can tempt him with your classes. A full load of psychology and life sciences is a pretty rare offer. Do NOT tell him how much I am paying you!" He was jokingly adamant. Nick got up and snickered his way out of Mr. Benson's office.

On Tuesday, as he stood up to teach his first class, Elizabeth raised her hand. "Yes, Elizabeth."

She stood up. Normally this was not required, but she did anyway. "We are hearing a disturbing rumor that you are retiring at the end of this quarter. Is that true?"

He stepped forward and sat on the edge of his desk, something he rarely did. "Yes, it's not a rumor, but the truth."

"Why? Have we been bad?" she almost whimpered.

"No, no, no, you are all wonderful. Many of you know that I am also an author. It's just time for the next chapter in my own life." As usual, his voice had a calming effect on the class.

Jude stood up, "Does this have something to do with losing your wife and daughters?"

"Good question, Jude." He said that a lot. If I hadn't lost them, I probably wouldn't be retiring yet, but now that they are gone it's time for the next chapter."

Jude had not given up, "Anything we could say or do to change your mind?"

"No, but thanks for asking. Now, we still have a lot of important things to cover during the rest of the quarter. Let's dive in." His enthusiasm certainly was not waning. Each new period followed a similar pattern. He had to answer some questions about his rumored retirement before he could begin the day's lesson.

For his last period, he began with. "Yes, the rumors of my retirement at the end of this quarter are true. It has nothing to do with you or the school. I love you all. It's just time for me to begin the next chapter in my life. And, no, there is nothing you can do to dissuade me, but thanks for wanting to. Okay? Let's get into today's lesson."

On his way home he stopped at the church. He had called Tom to make sure he was there as often the staff took the first part of the week off, having 'worked' all Saturday and Sunday. Tom's door was open, so he just went in. Tom sat behind his desk, a number of books open in front of him. "Nick, have a seat. What's up?"

Nick took a seat, "A number of things actually. I feel like I'm supposed to start a new chapter, now that Ann and the kids are gone."

Tom got up, came around the desk and sat in another chair facing Nick, "Like what?"

Nick crossed his legs, got relaxed and began, "For starters, I'm retiring at the end of this quarter."

Tom's eyes widened, "Wow, that is a big step." He let Nick continue.

"Then I'm going to get the house ready to sell while I move into the house next door. It's smaller and will require a lot less upkeep."

"That's true," Tom agreed, "your wife's landscaping practically requires a full-time gardener."

"So, I'd appreciate your prayers on all this and I also would like to ask you a favor."

"Name it," Tom added with enthusiasm.

"I have quite a lot of books. I'd like to start a library here at the church." He looked at Tom directly, "What do you think?"

Tom met his gaze, "Isn't that interesting. I just recently mentioned to the staff that it would be a real benefit to the congregation to have a good Christian library here. I think that Somebody has been preparing the ground work for you. I think we even have a good room identified that will provide convenient access at virtually all times of the week.

Nick breathed a sigh of relief, "That takes a load off my mind. I would, of course, help set it up, but do you have any ideas on who could manage it?"

"That's interesting too," Tom added. "In our last 'Introductions' class a gal named Ruth Tiddle joined us and she is a retired librarian looking for a way to serve the congregation. I'll give her a call. She would probably like to help you set it up too."

"*This just keeps getting better,*" Nick mused. "Yes, have her give me a call."

Tom nodded, "I will. Anything else?"

"Nope, I think that's it for now. Do you have time to pray right now?"

"You bet." Together they spent some time in prayer, shook hands and Nick left for home.

That night he got a call from Ruth Tiddle, "Hello Nick. This is Ruth Tiddle. Pastor Tom said that you'd be interested in starting a Christian library at the church. How can I help?"

It took a moment for Nick to get over the shock. "Thanks for calling. I have a couple of walls of floor-to-ceiling bookcases of books. Maybe you and your husband could come over some night, take a look at them, and see how we should proceed."

Ruth laughed, "I'm single, but I could bring a gal friend with me if that would help."

He breathed a sigh of relief, "Yes, that would be great. What night would work for you?"

"Would Thursday night be okay, say 7:00?"

"That would be great. Here's my address." Part of Nick knew that this would be difficult, going through the books and remembering reading some of them to the girls or picturing Ann curled up on the couch with one of her novels. He resigned that it might require some moral support and he wondered if Muriel could help him get through this difficult task. So when he was finished, he called her. He wasn't sure it even completed its first ring.

"Hi Nick."

"Hi Muriel, how was your day?"

"Pretty much same-o-same-o at the hospital. How about you?"

"I told my principal that I was retiring at the end of the quarter." He paused. "He told me he thought I was fishing for a raise, but I told him I was serious. We chatted a bit until I think he understood. The rumor spread quickly and I had to explain my reasoning at the beginning of each of the rest of my class periods. They were supportive, but sad that I was really going to be leaving."

"That must have been at least encouraging? No petitions were circulated saying. 'Stop Mr. Nick from leaving'? They will probably show up tomorrow," she joked.

"Right," he responded, unconvinced. "I also stopped at church on the way home and Tom fully supported my library idea. He even had a gal call me and set up a meeting Thursday night to look at my books at 7:00. Would you be interested in an early dinner on Thursday and being here with me when Ruth and her friend show up?"

"Sure, I could be ready by 5:30. Would that work?"

"Terrific, be thinking about where you would like to eat."

She laughed out loud, "I don't think we can get to Tahiti and back by 7:00."

Nick added his laughter, "Tahitian food. I'll see what I can do. Okay, I'm off to review my final quarter of classes. Have a great evening."

"You too, thanks."

Nick got his electric teapot going, a cup of instant decaf ready with sugar, and then went to his office to get tomorrow's planning papers out. He arranged them on his desk and got back to the kitchen just as the pot signaled that the water was ready. He poured a steaming cup of water into the cup, added some cream from the refrigerator, stirred it, and headed back to his office.

Tomorrow's lesson looked at "value," both intrinsic and extrinsic value, how they were defined, measured, and the roles they played in your life. He saw it as a pivotal, crucial lesson, and wanted it to touch the heart of each and every student. He spent some time in prayer before he reviewed the lesson, asking God to identify ways he could make it more special and pointed as he delivered it. He had done the class often, but he still wanted it to be special to tomorrow's students. He listened, pondered, and took notes on some new ideas that floated to the surface. He usually used the five qualities of determining value in gems: color, clarity, cut, flawlessness, and rarity, but today he he thought about the elegance of programming code, the efficient use of variables and sub-routines. He'd have to think and pray about it some more, but for some reason it seemed to powerfully resonate. By the time he got to 10:00 pm he also had something relating to cooking; the combining of spices that produced the exact flavor desired in contrast to the general use of salt and pepper. Salt and pepper seemed so common but added a great deal to everything's flavor. He went to bed pleased with what he had.

Chapter Nineteen: Finding Value and Starting a Library

He began his Tuesday's class with, "We have heard the old adage that, 'Beauty is in the eye of the beholder,' but what is beauty? How would you define it?"

Nolan raised his hand. "Nolan?"

"I'm not sure that I can define it. I think it produces a feeling, so that you know it when you see it."

Nick went on, "Is it different for different people?"

Nolan continued, "Probably."

"Good answer." Nick waited a moment. "Today's lesson is about value. How would you define value? What makes something valuable?"

Al raised his hand in the back of the room. "How much someone is willing to pay for it?"

Nick laughed, "Is that a question?"

The class tittered, but Al went on, "Ah, no, a statement of fact?"

"Still sounded like a question, Al, but we'll take your word for it. Are there characteristics to value?"

Al piped up, "Not sure?" to more twitters.

"In a gem, value is determined by color, clarity, cut, flawlessness, and rarity. How many of you are in Mr. Randolf's programing class?" Five hands went up. "What is elegant code?" One of the hands stayed up, although wavering a bit, "Karen?"

She spoke softly, "I think it is the ability to achieve your intended purpose in as few lines of code as possible."

"Very good, Karen. Now, did you catch that last part? Karen, when I said, 'Very good Karen,' how did you feel?"

She looked down at her desk and said softly, "Valued."

"Yes, acknowledgment and praise affirm value. Have you ever been in a class where no one will raise their hand and answer the question?" A number of heads nodded. "Why is that?"

Karen again spoke softly, "They are afraid of being criticized, ridiculed, shown to be wrong, devalued."

"Yes again, Karen. Those all detract or negate value. Do you ever feel like that in my class?" Virtually the entire class shook their head no. "And why is that?"

It was Karen again, "Because we know you value each and every one of us."

It brought tears to his eyes and he choked up as he said, "Yes, and I'm glad you all know it!" He waited a moment to regain his compsure. "We live in a society and culture of 'devaluement.'" He cocked his head to one side, "Not sure if that's a word, but it is refreshingly wonderful to be valued." There were many nodding their heads. "In your notebooks, list some of the other ways you can show a person that they are valuable." He sat on the edge of his desk, watched them work, thinking and writing, and breathed a quiet word of thanks to God.

In the next class he used the cooking example. It was Alphonso who answered the question. He almost never spoke in class, so it was extra special that he was the one Nick was allowed to value and affirm in front of the whole class.

The entire day had been wonderful. It seemed they had totally forgotten that in a few short weeks he would be retiring. In reality, they had not forgotten at all. A number of them formed groups after class, comparing their value lists, trying to determine how they would share with Mr. Nick how much he had meant to them.

Nick walked through the door of his house to a ringing telephone. It was Muriel, calling to see how his day went. She loved calling him because, even with all of the recent trauma in his life, he was still so incredibly upbeat. He was like a shot of adrenaline into her life. He had a chance to share with her all the wonders of his day teaching 'Value' to his students and how he had been able to touch some of them deeply.

He had just gotten off the phone with Muriel when his phone rang again. It was Rolf, the IT guy at church. He wanted Nick to know that he was building a database to house the library books. He would just need some simple data on each book. He assumed they would use the old Dewey Decimal system to categorize them. Then he would need the book's title, author, and he would print a QR code for each book. A person would just need to scan the code on their phone, add their name and email address, and the database would take care of the rest. Nearing the end of the thirty-day loan period, the database would send them an email reminder that the book was due back in the library. The database could also be used to search for books by category, title, or author. Nick sat there astounded. What a great idea. He thanked Rolf profusely.

Wednesday's classes were pretty simple and straightforward. He had a few people share one of their 'Value list' suggestions and then divided them into groups to create categories and develop other ways and means of showing value to people. Then he had the groups share with the class. Each group had to share something different, so it was in your best interest to go first. They came up with a lot of great and unique ideas.

When he got home, he separated out all of the books that he was going to keep. Then he started to collect books into boxes of categories by author. He started with fiction and went thru his three bookcases pulling all those books together. He had over forty books that he and Ann had collected that were just of Christian fiction. Next, he did language studies and helps. He then got an email from Rolf with a link to the database and an input form that he had developed for adding the books to the database.

Wow, this was going to make things so much easier. Rolf also explained that he had a printer that would print the QR code label for each book once it was in the database.

Just then Nick got an email from Pastor Tom. A room had been assigned as the library. Doug, a retired contractor at the church, wanted to meet to discuss its layout.

Nick gave Doug a call, "I hear that you are up for a little remodel job?" and he laughed.

Doug sounded pretty enthused, "Yup, They have given us two rooms on the east side of the building. I'll send you the current layout of the rooms so you will at least know the size of what we have to work with."

"Great!" Doug's enthusiasm was catchy. "I'm meeting with what will probably become the library committee tomorrow. Could we meet with you on Friday to chat about options?"

"Sure, wanna meet at the church about 7:00, I have keys to the building."

"That sounds good, I'll confirm it after I've talked to the committee, but hopefully I'll see you then," and Nick hung up.

After his supper, Muriel called him before he could call her. Her day was pretty uneventful, but he had a chance to share with her how things were moving ahead on the library.

"Have you thought about where you would like to go to dinner?" he asked.

"What do you think of Arby's?" she asked tentatively.

He snickered, "It's not chicken," and paused, "but I like it just fine. I even think I have some coupons."

"You use coupons?" She sounded surprised.

"Sure, save where and whenever you can. That's my motto."

"Wonderful, I'll see you at 5:30 tomorrow?"

"Yup, I'll be there with bells on." Then he added, "Not literally."

She guffawed and said goodnight.

Thursday was a beautiful late spring evening and Muriel sat on the bench of her front porch as Nick drove up. He was still in his suit and tie from school, she was in a spring dress. While a simple flowered pink dress, it arrested his attention none the less.

"Wow!" He took a deep breath, "Have you been waiting long?"

She cocked her head slightly to the left, "No, silly. It's just 5:30 and I know how prompt you are. I sat here a moment ago." She rose from the bench, "Ready?"

"Yup," and he walked up her porch and offered her his arm, which she took.

"Then, on to our next adventure," and they nearly skipped to the car. As always, he opened her door for her, she swished into her seat, pulling her skirt in behind her so he didn't close it in the door. They were at Arby's in a jiffy. "Drive-through or the dining room?"

"Do we have time for the dining room?"

"We do," and he pulled into a parking spot, jumped out to open and close her car door and open the door to Arby's. At 5:35 there was only a young family seated in the dining room. They stepped up to the counter as the cashier asked, "What can I get started for you?"

Nick turned to Muriel for her order, "A roast beef sandwich, fries, and," she winked at Nick, "a chocolate shake."

"Hmm, a big spender tonight. I'll have two roast beef sandwiches, fries, and a Jamocha shake, thank you. Oh, I have coupons."

The cashier took the coupons, punched some selections into her computer, and quoted him the total. Nick handed her a twenty and some coins, received his change, and they stepped aside to wait for their order.

"Name for the order?" The cashier asked.

"Nick," Nick responded. He turned to Muriel and whispered, "I almost wore my Chick-fil-A cap tonight but decided not to chance it. Some people are offended when I wear it in their restaurant, others feel a sense of pride that I have chosen to eat at their place instead of at my own."

Another waitress called out, "Nick," and placed their tray on the counter. They took the tray to the condiments table and doctored up their sandwiches, grabbed straws for the shakes, and walked to a booth.

Muriel started, "My day started pretty uneventfully, but it turned into 'cancer' day. I had one patient after another come in on their way to surgery or oncology prior to treatment. I so wanted to tell my story, but I still have to wait for tomorrow's confirmation. Then I will send all the cancer patients to you."

Nick held up his hands, "Wait, just a minute."

She laughed lightly, "I know. You were just an instrument, but a Stradivarius is still the finest violin on the planet."

Nick looked down at the table as she reached over to take his hand, "I feel more like just a plain old fiddle," and he laughed lightly too.

"What about your day?" she probed inquisitively.

Nick shrugged his shoulders, "Much of my life seems to be 'getting ready.' Getting ready to retire, getting ready to sell my house, getting ready to start a new library at the church." He chuckled. "This is not just a way of saying, 'Expect my house to be messy,' right now it will seem so. I am usually pretty tidy." He chuckled again. "I have been well trained." He paused, "I did start getting some of my books ready, so we have something concrete to chat about tonight. Rolf, the IT guy at church, has built a database to ease our inputting of the books, our tracking them, checking them out, etc. He will even be able to print QR codes for each book that will only need to be scanned on the way out of the library, plus the person's name and email address, and then back in when the books are returned."

They picked up what was left of their shakes, put their sandwich wrappers and empty fry boxes on the tray, and discarded it all in the trash receptacles on the way out to Nick's car. They parked in the back by Nick's detached garage, and he showed her the backyard on the way to the back door. It was really quite impressive, the lawn, the flowerbeds, a beautiful fountain, and pool. Nick's wife, Ann, had what the Chinese called 'feng shui,' the ability to create environments of peace and harmony. It almost took Muriel's breath away and then returned it to her four-fold. In the middle the back yard was what Nick affectionately called, the 'four hundred pound lawn bench,' that was covered in Jasmine. It was nearly intoxicating. They sat on the bench and finished their milkshakes in silence. Then Nick took Muriel in the back door of his home.

Chapter Twenty:
The Library Committee

The house was a two-story Craftsman built in the early 1900's. Nick and Muriel entered through what used to have been the back porch, but had been remodeled into a laundry room that also contained the chest freezer. The kitchen had been enlarged to contain a small dining area, separate from the formal dining room. Beyond the formal dining room she found a spacious living room with a freestanding fireplace. A wooden arch led into the entryway and the first of the floor-to-ceiling bookcases. It was over four feet wide and took up most of the entire wall that separated the entryway from the living room. The other wall abutted the stairs and contained a coat closet. Between the two walls and opposite the front door was the downstairs bathroom. In the original house it had been the kitchen's pantry, but since then it had served several purposes until Ann wanted it turned into a bathroom.

"It should be easy," she had said. "The plumbing is right there in the wall." That became Nick's response to most of Ann's requested "easy" projects, "Sure, the plumbing's right there in the wall."

Upstairs on the right they encountered a compact bathroom opposite the kids' room on the left. After the kids' room was Nick's office and a lot more books. Across from the office was what had been Nick and Ann's bedroom. Off of it, a former walk-in closet housed Ann's office and another wall of books. That completed the tour, less the attic and under-eve storage areas. It was a very nice house and you could still feel Ann's hand everywhere. He hadn't changed much since the accident, but it was so difficult to see reminders of them everywhere he looked. He knew that part of moving on would require him to begin making more changes. Still, it would be difficult to do, especially alone. They went back downstairs to heat up some water for coffee and tea.

The doorbell rang right at 7:00 and Nick ushered in Ruth and her friend. Ruth had been a public librarian. Her friend Nicole, they found out, had been a high school librarian. The four of them sat around the small kitchen table. It appeared to be oak, as were the chairs. The cushions, a light blue floral pattern, matched the color of the kitchen. Nick had a number of materials to pass out as he spoke. He began with a layout of the proposed library.

"Wow!" Ruth exclaimed, "You have already done a lot of thinking about this. Talk us through what you have here."

Nick began with the two empty rooms that Doug had given him and proceeded to show them how he had designed one to be full of books and bookcases and the other with facilities for searching for books, checking them out, returning them, and even donating new volumes. It also contained a place to read, study and to complete administrative duties.

Nick set up his flat screen on the counter behind himself to project from his laptop and he showed them the database that Rolf had designed. He brought it up via the QR code and then showed how they would input the books. Rolf would print a QR code for each book that would make it easy for them to be checked out and returned. He walked them through the example of a book that Rolf had already input. Again, Ruth and Nicole were pleased at the forethought and preparation that had already been done

Nick sighed, "So, questions, comments, improvements? I don't want you to think this is a done deal or my baby. I want it to be ours and just wanted us to have something to start with. Nothing's cast in stone. I scheduled a meeting tomorrow night with Rolf and Doug, assuming we agree on what we want."

Church Library Layout

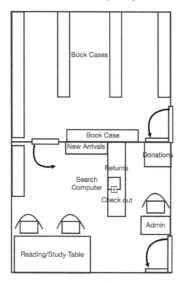

Ruth smiled, "I really appreciate all the work you have put into this. I do have a couple of suggestions. First, since most of the traffic will occur around the front desk, it might be better to move the study table into the other room where it will remain quieter." She looked at Nicole, "What do you think?"

Nicole considered what Ruth had said and then responded, "I would tend to agree with Ruth. Do you have the layout on your computer and can we try moving things around a bit?"

"Sure," and Nick brought the layout up on the screen.

Muriel contributed, "If we want the second room to become more of a reading room, maybe you could add a couch here," and she pointed to the screen.

"And move the table there," Ruth pointed out.

"Move bookcases back to the first room," Nicole pointed out, "then most of the books and commotion would be relegated to the first room. What do you think?" Nick movedd the icons around and they all looked at the finished product.

Nick said, "I like it. The second room could double as a meeting room for a book club or meeting of the library committee.

They all nodded, *"Yes."*

Church Library Layout Rev.

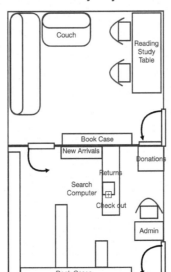

"What other concerns did you have?" Nick asked Ruth.

"Are we worried about items being stolen?" She smiled slightly.

Nick returned the smile, "Well, I don't think there is a huge market for stolen Christian literature, and it might do the thief good if they read it. So, probably not."

Nicole interjected, "Will the current layout provide enough bookcases for the projected inventory?"

Nick looked off into the distance, "I think for the foreseeable future. We can always add more bookcases to the reading room."

Ruth still smiled, "Then I think we should pray and proceed." Nick nodded and Ruth prayed.

"Can I consider us to be the library committee?" They all nodded. "Would any of you like to accompany me when I meet with Doug the carpenter and Rolf our IT guy?" Both Ruth and Nicole nodded again. "Okay, I have a tentative meeting tomorrow evening at 7:00. I will confirm that and get back to you."

They both said, almost in unison, "Perfect."

They finished their coffee and tea around some small talk. Ruth had only recently begun to attend the church. Nicole had been there for a few years, but attended the second service so their paths had not crossed, although she did recall one of the church plays he had been in. He had played Pontus Pilate so well that most people had despised him, or at least his character. That is the true test of an actor; when you play a villain and make the people forget it's you and hate the character. Nick had passed the test.

Nick and Muriel walked them to their car and then went around back and Nick took Muriel home. He walked her to her door, which she unlocked, turned and stood in the soft porch light. "Thank you for letting me accompany you in this new chapter of your life." She then laughed, "I know, 'Your pleasure,' right?"

"Yup, that about says it all." He stepped forward and gave her a hug. She put her head on his shoulder and lingered.

Chapter Twenty-One:
The Library Construction

Nick had just walked into his home and put his briefcase down when the phone rang. It was Muriel, "Big plans for the evening?"

"If you will recall I have a meeting with the guy who will construct the library at 7:00," he reminded her.

"You do still need to eat don't you?" she jovially inquired.

He sighed, but was actually excited, "I guess so."

"How about my place at 5:30?" Her voice still sounded tinged with joy.

He was surprised, "Ah sure. I'll see you then."

Nick took a quick shower, dressed in business casual, grabbed a copy of the library layout and left for Muriel's.

She opened the door before he could knock on it, "Hi, Big guy. Come on in. You can open the wine, but only a half a glass for you, you're driving."

They walked into the kitchen where she had a small dining room table set for two. No candles, but everything else looked faintly romantic. The bottle of wine sat near two goblets and an opener. He wondered if he should pretend he didn't know how to open the bottle, but decided just to open it. He poured a glass for her, then as instructed only half a glass for himself. It appeared to be a nice Riesling.

He sat at the table and soaked up the ambience of what she had created. She set a plate of two steaks in front of him. One had a plastic label sticking out of it indicating that it was cooked medium, the other was medium well. "Your choice," and she indicated the steaks then joined them with a bowl of steaming mashed potatoes and a small bowl of cooked peas. "Butter or margarine?"

He put the medium steak on his plate as he smiled, "Butter, please."

She went to the refrigerator and returned with the butter tray and set it on the table. She sat and asked, "Would you like to offer thanks?"

He began, actually choked up a bit, "I'm so happy I could cry. Thank You and thank you," and he looked Muriel in the eyes.

Her eyes crinkled as she replied, "My pleasure."

He just shook his head from side to side.

She reached out her hand across the table and he took it, "I had my doctor's appointment."

Nick's eyes widened as he held her hand more tightly. "And?"

A tear glistened in the corner of her eye, "I'm cancer free."

He reached out for her other hand which she took, "That's wonderful!"

A smile crinkled her eyes too, "Can I send all my cancer patients to you now that it's confirmed? You can play the fiddle for them."

He shook his head from side to side, "No, I think He operates more on a case-by-case basis, rather than waving a magic wand over all of them." He paused to listen to another 'still small voice,' "Unless you feel a special prompting, then I suppose you could call me and we both could meet with them."

"Hmmm," she intoned, "an interesting proposition," and she squeezed his hands again.

During the rest of their supper they shared the ordinary joys and the challenges of the day. Then together they took their dishes to the sink, and she filled the dishwasher. That only left the pots and pans used in preparing the meal. With her permission he dried what she washed, with only the clanking of the pans to break the silence. They left in plenty of time to get to the church before seven and sat there in the parking lot.

Nick sighed, "Life is sure different than I thought it would be at this point."

She put her hand on top of his, "Mine too." He turned his hand over and they interlocked fingers. He gave her hand a little squeeze and then she removed it and put it back in her lap. She turned in her seat and asked, "So, what are your intentions concerning us?"

He turned towards her, "That's a good question. One we should ponder and pray about answering."

"Let's do that," and she folded her hands.

Nick laughed, "Do I have to close my eyes too? You know that has nothing to do with praying other than helping some people concentrate."

She smiled back, "I suppose we can talk to Him like He's right here, because He is?"

"Yup," Nick still laughed slightly. They talked to Him for a few minutes and then two other cars pulled up. They assumed it was Doug, Ruth, and maybe Nicole. They got out, shared introductions all around, including handshakes, and Doug unlocked the door to the church building.

He took them upstairs to the two rooms that had been identified. In one he had a table and a couple chairs. They had to scramble to find some more, but soon four of them were seated around the table.

Doug still stood, "I'll be right back after I turn on the electric teapot to warm us up some water," and he left. He returned shortly with a tray of cups, instant coffee, assorted tea bags, sugars, and creamers like they served on Sunday mornings. "I should be right back with the water," and he was true to his word.

"Now, if someone would pray, we can select our poison and begin."

Nick did, they mixed their drinks and reviewed the revised library layout.

Ruth walked Doug through the flow of the first room and the purpose of the second. He was suitably impressed. "I think I can have the rooms ready by month's end. How soon can you have the books catalogued, input, and on the shelves?

They looked at each other and nodded.

"I think we can support that," Nick ventured and picked up his phone. He called Rolf, "I hope I'm not disturbing you at home, but where can I pick up some QR code label printers?"

Rolf answered him and he repeated it to the rest of them, "It just so happens they are on sale at the local big box electronics store this month."

Nick thanked him and hung up, "I'll bring each of you a printer and a box of books on Sunday. Do you have any preference on what you are categorizing?" They looked at each other and shook their head no. "Doug, any problem with the sofa, table and chairs?"

Doug shook his head, "We get donations all the time. I'll look to see what's available, but I'm pretty sure we'll be okay."

"Anything else?" They all shook their heads again. "Nicole, could you close us in prayer please?" She did.

Muriel offered, "I could type up some minutes of this meeting, include the layout, and email it to pastor Tom, if you'd like."

Nick sighed, "That would be wonderful. Thanks."

Doug put everything back on the tray and headed off to the kitchen, while the rest of them left the building and went to their cars.

As they stood by their cars, Ruth commented, "Well, that was productive. Seems sort of easy to see His hand in this, doesn't it?" They agreed. Then a look of concern crossed Ruth's face as she pointed beyond Nick.

A man stood in the shadows. He was on the other side of Nick's car and as Nick turned to face him, he stepped into the light.

"Jonathan, what are you doing here?"

His smile was disarming, and the threat vanished, "I was driving by, saw your car and thought I'd stop and say, 'Hi.'"

Nick turned back to the others, "This is my friend Jonathan, we met recently at Chick-fil-A. This is Muriel, Ruth, and Nicole. We are the new church library committee," and Nick laughed as though he had just made a joke.

Jonathan kept smiling. "And how are things, Nick?"

Nick looked off to the left, "They are surprisingly wonderful. Thanks for asking."

"Will you be at Chick-fil-A in the morning?" he asked.

Nick thought, "Saturday, yup. Will I see you there?"

"I think you will, nice to meet you all," and he turned to his car.

Nick was shocked, "Is that yours?" It was a small, two-passenger, three-wheeled electric car.

"Yup, they only made a few thousand of them and then had to recall them all for a fatal engineering flaw. I fixed mine. It's a lot of fun to drive." Jonathan smiled mischievously, "If you're good, maybe I'll let you take it for a spin in the morning."

It was like Nick had just been promised a chance to play with a new toy, "Really?"

"If you're good," and he snickered.

"Okay, I'll see you in the morning."

They all said good-bye, got in their cars and headed their separate ways. On the way to drop Muriel off, Nick went on and on about the little three-wheeled electric car he had always wanted to have.

Chapter Twenty-Two: Saturday Morning at Chick-fil-A

Nick was up even early for him. He dressed and had his morning devotional time. He read a chapter in Proverbs until something jumped out at him. Then he reflected on it with Him for a few moments using the SOAP method: Scripture, Observation, Application, Prayer. This morning he had been in the seventeenth chapter, verses thirty-one and two:

Scripture: Proverbs 16:31-32 *Gray hair is a crown of glory when gained in righteous living. Whoever is slow to anger is better than the mighty, and he who rules his spirit than the hero.*

Observation: There is a reason to seek first righteousness and that the last fruit of the spirit is self-control. To be complete you must practice both.

Application: While righteousness is a gift and self-control a fruit, both must be practiced to make any difference in my living.

Prayer: Help me to receive and live what You give, until it is seen in my daily life.

He was so excited that he got to Chick-fil-A a full ten minutes before it opened. At least that gave him a few minutes to calm down. Jonathan's little electric car was nowhere to be seen. He went in, ordered on the App, got out his iPad mini with its portable keyboard, and began working on his Christmas novel. He was nearly through with it.

Led by the angel Uriel, the Magi, the lady, and the soldier were about to meet the two-year-old, new King of the Jews. They approached the house where reportedly a carpenter, his wife, and young son lived. Although late in the evening, the lights were still on, and they had reason to believe that they were expected. They dismounted from their horses and walked to the door. Uriel stepped forward, knocked on the door, and stepped back. A young woman opened the door. It was like meeting Abigail all over again. They fought the desire to fall on their knees.

"*Who is this woman?*" they all asked themselves.

Then from behind her they heard, "Who is it, Momma?" The sound of his voice did drive them all to their knees, as the young child stepped to his mother's side and took her hand.

An older man stepped up behind the two of them and said, "Welcome, please come into our home and be blessed."

Nick looked up to find Jonathan standing there, tray in hand. He had no idea how long he'd been standing there.

Jonathan answered his unasked question, "Not long. You seemed lost to the world."

"Sorry, I'm in the last chapters of my current novel, *The Magi and a Lady*." He shook his head, trying to come back to the present.

"No problem, you can continue while I finish my breakfast if you'd like." Jonathan was always so considerate, one of his many endearing qualities.

"Naw, that's okay. I'm at a good stopping place," Nick countered.

"So, the library committee?" Jonathan probed.

"Yeah, we're going to start a library there at the church building. Part of my 'simplify life and get ready to sell my house' includes finding a place for my old personal library," Nick explained.

"Hmm, sounds like a good idea," and Jonathan ate his last bite.

"I mean, I was only contemplating it earlier in the week and 'Bam!' It's a done deal. Somebody else musta been planning this for a while."

Jonathan chuckled, "It is funny how smoothly some things can go and how difficult other things seem to be."

Just then Ranae, the owner, stepped from out of nowhere and up to their table. She had a large bag in her hand. She addressed them, "Nick, Jonathan. It's good to see you both." Nick started to rise but she held out the bag and blocked his way. "I hear you stopped a robber from taking advantage of us."

Nick pointed upward, "I obviously had some help."

She continued, "Well, we got you something as our way of saying thanks." She held out the bag.

Nick took it, set it next to him and looked inside. His eyes widened. He brought out a Chick-fil-A jacket and hat, and tears formed in his eyes.

"Try it on,"

He got up on the other side of his chair and put the jacket on.

"Hmmm, looks great. Check in the pocket."

He did and found a name badge. It said, "Mr. Nick, Our CFA Hero."

Now a tear did trickle down his face as he said, "Thank you."

She of course responded characteristically, "Our pleasure, have a great day. You too, Jonathan." She turned and left them alone.

"Wow, a new hat and now a jacket too." Nick took out his handkerchief, dabbed at his eyes, and blew his nose.

"A name tag too. Maybe you should start charging for the bathroom code?" Jonathan chuckled.

Nick took a slow breath and changed the subject, "So, tell me about your little electric car."

Jonathan beamed, "I really like it. It's nimble, has some zip, and is a lot of fun to drive. Would you like to take it for a spin?"

Nick displayed mock concern, "Is it safe?"

Jonathan returned the look, "Would I let you in it if it wasn't?"

"Point taken, sure, let's go for a drive. Should we get a refill of our drinks first?"

"There are cup holders although you'd wonder where they could put them." Jonathan picked up his tray and headed for the garbage machine with Nick close behind him. They then refreshed their drinks and headed out to the car.

Nick looked at Jonathan, "Surely you're not going to fit into that back seat?"

Jonathan smiled, "It's not a problem as long as you are flexible and not in a hurry."

The seating in the car was tandem, like the cockpit of a jet. Jonathan opened the front door, reached in to flip a switch and the front seat tilted forward. He climbed into the back, placing his drink in the cupholder along the way, and sat down. Nick expected him to put on his copilot's helmet next, but he just buckled up.

Nick climbed into the driver's seat. It was easier than it looked. He closed the door, buckled up and looked for his pilot's helmet.

Jonathan asked, "What are you looking for?"

Nick spoke with mock sincerity, "My flight helmet."

Jonathan could not be seen in the rear-view mirror. There wasn't one, just two side mirrors. He shook his head anyway, "There isn't one."

Nick reached his hand back alongside the seat towards Jonathan's knee. "Now what," Jonathan asked, trying not to sound exasperated.

"Keys?" It seemed a reasonable request.

"They're in my pocket. You don't need them. Just step on the brake and push the start button." Nick pushed the button and nothing happened except the screen in front of him activated. "You may find this unsettling because there is no engine noise.

On the console to your right push the button marked "Brake." Then the "R" for reverse." Nick did so and the screen filled with the image from the backup camera. It contained an image of the car and behind it a number of yellow rectangles stretching the width of the car and backwards. The last rectangle was red. "If you back up until something enters the red rectangle, you will have hit it."

Nick backed up, turned around, and headed out of the parking lot. "Can I take it on the freeway?"

"You can do whatever you'd like, as long as we are back in time for you to make your next appointment." Jonathan was no longer exasperated.

Nick wanted to say, "Yippee," but held it back. "Okay."

The car was a lot of fun to drive. As advertised it was both nimble and zippy. It was small though and gave Nick a little bit of concern on the freeway. Would other cars be able to see him? It seemed they could. They had no problems. They turned around and were back to Chick-fil-A in plenty of time for Nick to head home and start the laundry for the week.

Chapter Twenty-Three: Aberrant Behavior

It was Monday morning. His first class after breakfast at Chick-fil-A. Since this would be the final quarter he taught before he retired, he was pulling out all the stops. This last section was on aberrant behavior in the abnormal psychology section. Last week he had covered suicide. It had been pivotal, resulting in a number of kids coming to talk to him both during and after school.

He began, "Today's topic is Human Trafficking, the second largest revenue producing criminal activity on the planet. It is second only to drugs." He paused for emphasis, "You can sell cocaine once, but a person can be resold again and again and again. One of the key things you need to know is how to recognize an abduction. One way involves knowing the universal hand sign for 'Help me, I'm in trouble.'" He showed them the hand sign, making a fist with your thumb inside of your gripping fingers, then opening and closing the fingers.

He remembered the evening that he taught his own girls this hand sign after supper. He caught them once using it to try and get out of drying the dishes and made sure they understood, after that little incident, that it was something very serious and only to be used when in real danger. They understood and apologized.

He continued, "This is something every parent should teach their children and something everyone here should know. It is going to be difficult to be 'upbeat' about the topic of 'Human Trafficking,'" he paused, "but I will try." There was weak laughter.

Nick turned to the whiteboard, "At any one time there are nearly thirty million victims of human trafficking. These fall into two categories: forced labor and commercial sex. Forced labor occurs all across the planet; from hotels to massage parlors, from a burger joint to what appears to be a fine restaurant, from the farm to the rice fields, and to many places we would just call sweat shops. Commercial sex trafficking is similar. It's everywhere, and the biggest consumer of sex trafficking? It's the good old US of A. What can we do? That's a good question. Get into your personality groups and answer that question."

Just before the bell rang ending class, Nick said, "Tomorrow we will share the ways you answered that question. Have a good day and see you tomorrow." The class somberly shuffled out of the room.

On his way home that afternoon, Nick stopped by the grocery store. A nicely dressed man, probably in his forties, and a young girl walked out of the store holding hands. *"Probably his granddaughter,"* he thought. The girl caught his eye. Nick looked down at her hand and she was making the universal sign for *"Help me!"*

"You're kidding," he thought as he pulled out his phone, dialed 911, put his phone to his ear, and turned around to hear, "911, what is your emergency?"

Nick responded, "Get the police, I am witnessing a child abduction," and he called out loudly to the man, "Sir!" The man turned around and Nick pointed the phone towards him, "I have the police on the line, release the girl."

The man was stunned for a moment. He looked at Nick, then the phone, back to Nick. He let go of the girl's hand and Nick held out his own. The girl ran to grab Nick's hand. The man reached under the left armpit of his coat like he might be going for a gun in a shoulder holster, stopped, then turned and walked away. Nick watched him get into a car and back out of a parking spot. Nick flipped his phone into camera mode and took a photo of the license plate.

Nick heard his phone say, "Sir, are you still there?"

Nick took a deep breath, "Yes, I am. I have the girl, and I got his license plate."

The voice on the phone responded, "I have an officer on the way. You are at," and then named the grocery store.

"Yes, we are here and will wait for the officer." There was a bench in front of the store. They went over and sat on it.

The phone responded, "He's about two minutes out. Is there anything else I can do for you?"

"No, and thank you." Nick looked at the little girl.

The 911 operator said, "You're welcome. Sir, what you did was dangerous, but thank you too," and hung up.

Nick found that he was shaking. Probably the adrenaline wearing off. He looked at the girl again, "How old are you?"

She smiled. He was surprised that in this situation she could, "Seven."

"And your name?" He smiled weakly in return.

"Samantha. Are you one of the good guys?" She still smiled.

Nick laughed slightly, "I guess you could say so. A police officer is coming and then we will get you back to your parents."

She looked down, they were still holding hands. "My mommy is at work. I was hungry so I walked to the store."

Nick furrowed his brows, "You were home alone?" She nodded. "Do you know your address?" She nodded again.

A police car drove up, parked, an officer got out, and saw them on the bench. He approached and stuck out his hand to Nick, "Officer Donnelly. Is this the young lady?"

"Yes, officer. This is Samantha, she's seven, and was home alone."

"And you are?" It was difficult to discern the officer's mood.

The shaking was subsiding. "Nick Grant. I teach at the high school."

Finally, the officer smiled. "I thought I recognized you. You spoke at the PTA kick-off meeting this year."

Nick looked down bashfully, "I did, I usually do."

The officer paused, "You know that confronting a kidnapper is dangerous?"

Nick looked down again, "Probably why I am still shaking."

Officer Donnelly bent down to catch Nick's eyes, "But I'm glad you did."

His hands steadied a little. "He may have had a gun, but I got his license plate number and gave it to 911."

Officer Donnelly smiled, "Yup, we got it. Would you be able to identify him?" Nick nodded. "Could you come down to the station and work with our sketch artist to create a picture of him?" Nick nodded again. Officer Donnelly held out his hand, "Samantha, let's get you home." She leaned over and hugged Nick, got up, and took Officer Donnelly's hand.

She smiled brightly, "Thank you Mr. Nick."

Nick returned the smile, "My pleasure," and laughed at his own little joke. Nick pulled out his business card: "Story-teller, Creating, Writing, Acting, Teaching, presenting stories to promote transformation." It contained his email and his cell phone number. He gave it to the officer to give to her parents.

She said, "Bye," and paused, then again, "Thank you," and waved.

He nodded and turned towards the grocery store. Shopping would be rather anticlimactic.

Chapter Twenty-Four: Date Night Dinner

After his little adventure at the grocery store, Nick called Muriel and told her about Samantha and his thwarting of her abduction. While concerned about the dangerous position he had put himself into, she was grateful that it had all turned out okay.

For most of the time that Nick and Ann had been married, Friday night had been designated as "Date Night" and they would at least go out to dinner. Nick took a breath, then asked Muriel out to dinner that Friday evening. She gleefully accepted. She then told him of her comparatively uneventful day at admissions.

Tuesday morning, while at his normal table for breakfast, Nick looked up to find Jonathan standing there, "May I join you?"

It was always wonderful to see Jonathan. "Yes. Please do."

Jonathan took his breakfast off his tray, place it on the table, took his tray to its place on top of the automated garbage receptacle, and returned to sit down. "I hear you had quite a day Monday afternoon."

"How did you hear about that?" Nick was surprised.

Jonathan continued, "Word on the street is that you foiled the abduction of a young girl." Nick's eyes widened even more. Jonathan chuckled, "I keep my ear to the ground. Either that or it's my vast network of spies. Are you attempting to win permanent hero status or some kind of award?" His chuckle lengthened.

Nick began to tell him the whole story with, "It was funny because just that day, in class, I had taught on that very thing. I had even shown them the universal hand-sign for 'Help, I'm in trouble.' Then, after school, I go to the grocery store, and a young girl gave me the hand sign on her way out of the store while holding the hand of a man. So, I called 911 and told him to let her go."

Jonathan interrupted, "Couldn't that have been dangerous?"

Nick looked over his head, "I suppose, but it seemed the right thing to do. He did reach under his coat like he might have had a gun, but he didn't draw it, just turned and left. I did get his license plate though and went down to the police station and worked with their sketch artist to capture a picture of him."

"Good for you," he tipped back on his chair and peeked around the corner to say, "Julie, we have a hero with us today. Mr. Nick."

She responded, "He's already foiled a robbery here, now what?"

Jonathan answered, "On Monday he foiled the abduction of a young girl."

Julie stepped up to the table and held out her hand for Nick to shake. "Can I offer the second-time-a-hero an ice cream cone reward?"

Nick was surprised, "For breakfast?"

Jonathan laughed out loud, "It's never too early for ice cream."

Nick let go of Julie's hand. "Sure, why not?" Julie returned with an ice cream cone and Nick and Jonathan chatted about what else was going on in their lives.

At school, Nick stopped by the office to check his mailbox and was greeted with, "It's the hero," by Betty the school's secretary.

Nick blushed, "Does everybody know about what happened yesterday?"

Betty smiled, "I think so."

As he got to his classroom there were already some students there. The word "HERO" was written on the board in large Calligraphy letters. He just stood there, looking at the board while students entered the classroom behind him. He walked to his desk and turned to face the class as the bell rang. Before he could say anything, they began clapping and standing, until the entire class stood there in raucous applause accompanied by whistles and catcalls. Embarrassed, Nick motioned for them to all sit down. Reluctantly they did.

He began, "Obviously, the word has gotten around about my little escapade yesterday at the grocery store."

Someone in the back of the class yelled, "Yes!" and the class laughed.

Nick looked down, "I'm not sure that makes me a hero, but what I do know is that the universal hand sign for 'Help! I'm in trouble!' made quite a difference to one young girl's life yesterday."

Someone in the back yelled again, "Hear, hear!"

He shook his head back and forth, *"Would the whole day be like this?"* then he said out loud, "Well, let's look at your lists of ways to stop trafficking and then we'll look at some other aberrant behavior and hope that this time it isn't prophetic." That got some more chuckles.

Friday evening, Muriel stood on her front porch, having just locked the front door. Nick got out of the car and went around to open the door for her as she walked down her sidewalk. She had dressed a little fancier as Nick had warned her that dinner was going to be a little more "upscale" tonight. They hugged briefly, she got in, he closed the door, and went around to get in on his own side, That's when he heard the shot or it might have been a firecracker. He stood by the side of his car, but nothing followed. He got in and closed the door, "Did you hear that?"

She didn't look alarmed, "Firecracker?"

Nick sighed, "Let's hope so." "*Maybe I'm getting paranoid,*" he thought. He started the car and off they went. "Have you ever been to 'Halley's Comet?'"

It was her turn to sigh as she smiled, "The one on the cliff overlooking the Bay? I haven't been there in a long time."

"Well, it's your lucky night, assuming your last experience there was positive." He looked at her questioningly.

"Now, it's you who is in luck. It was."

He ordered the seafood Alfredo and she the lasagna. Both were incredible. He had a glass of white wine and would keep himself to that single glass. Coupled with the food and length of their time in the restaurant, it should preclude the wine from impairing his driving. Although he had already told her about the thwarted abduction on Monday afternoon, she brought it up again. After he had stopped by the Precinct to help build the composite sketch, a reporter had caught him outside of the station and recorded a live interview. It had made the evening news. Now, he was a hero everywhere he went. It was quite embarrassing.

The food had been wonderful, their conversation light when suddenly there was a man standing at the table.

It was the abductor, with his hand in his coat pocket. "You are about to be a dead hero," he whispered through his teeth.

"Nope," Nick spoke nonchalantly, "have a seat and join us." Nick stood and held out his hand, "Nick."

"I know who you are. You were Monday evening's top story." His words dripped with anger.

Nick looked three tables over and spied Jonathan on his cell phone. "Sit down and have a glass of wine." His hand was still extended, Muriel looked rightfully puzzled. "Go ahead, sit down."

He brought his hand out of his coat pocket and took Nick's hand, "Jarvis," and sat down.

Nick raised his hand and caught the waiter's eye. He introduced Jarvis to Muriel and when the waiter approached, asked him for another wine glass.

Jarvis looked at the table then back to Nick, "What's the occasion?"

Nick smiled, "Nothing special, we don't usually eat this fancy, but thought we'd give it a whirl."

He looked at Muriel, "This your wife?" He had placed his hand back in his coat pocket.

"Nope," Nick answered with deliberate casualness, "we're just friends." He took a deep breath to brace himself, "My wife and two daughters were killed in a tragic car accident a short time ago."

Jarvis looked at the table again and the waiter brought his wine glass. Nick filled it and handed it to him as he gently said, "You have a few decisions to make."

Jarvis took the glass, a long pull of the wine, and looked directly into Nick's eyes.

"The police will be here shortly," Jarvis bristled, "and the easiest and best decision would be to let yourself be arrested. I think I can help you do that without making a scene." Nick paused, "Or you can stand up, shout, 'You'll never take me alive!' and go down in a hail of gunfire." The way Nick said it made the second option seem pretty foolish. "Can I have your gun?"

After an interminable pause, Jarvis slowly took the gun out of his pocket and handed it butt first to Nick under the table without anyone seeing it. "So, it will be option one?"

Jarvis nodded.

Nick looked to Jonathan who motioned with his head toward the door. "Just stay here and chat with Muriel, I'll be right back."

Nick got up and walked to where two officers were talking with the Maître d'. Nick looked at the officer's badge, "Officer Hadley, the man who tried to unsuccessfully abduct a young girl yesterday is sitting at my table. I have his gun in my pocket. He is willing to come with you without any trouble. May I go bring him to you?"

Officer Hadley looked at his partner then back to Nick, "You're kidding?"

"Nope," and Nick reached into his pocket, "Here's his gun." Nick discretely handed it to the officer.

"Wait, you're the guy who frustrated the abduction." Officer Hadley's eyes were wide.

"Guilty as charged. May I go get him for you? Oh, and I'd appreciate it if you didn't handcuff him until you were out of the restaurant."

Officer Hadley shrugged his shoulders, "Sure."

"Thanks," and Nick turned on his heel and walked back to the table. "Jarvis, wanna take one more drink of wine before you go?"

Jarvis took another long drink, emptying the glass.

Nick continued, "Two more things: there'll be no handcuffs until you are out of the restaurant," and Nick looked deep into Jarvis' eyes, "and I forgive you."

Tears formed in the corners of Jarvis' eyes, "You can do that?"

Nick smiled, "I just did," he said matter-of-factly.

Jarvis got slowly out of his chair and looked at Muriel, "Don't let this one go," and he pointed to Nick.

They walked to the officers and Nick pointed to Officer Hadley, "This is Officer Hadley," then back to Jarvis, "and this is Jarvis."

Jarvis could hardly believe it, but he offered his hand, "Officer?"

Officer Hadley could hardly believe it himself, but he took his hand, "Will you come with us, please."

Jarvis simply responded, "Yes, sir," and the three of them turned to leave.

"Jarvis," Nick called after them, "I'll come and visit if that's okay?"

Jarvis had turned back at the calling of his name, smiled weakly and responded, "I'd like that." Officer Hadley placed a hand on Jarvis' shoulder, turned him towards the exit and the three of them left the restaurant.

Nick stood there a moment, breathing slowly and deeply. He turned and scanned the restaurant. Jonathan was nowhere to be seen. Nick turned and sauntered back to the table. As he sat he asked, "Dessert?"

Muriel nodded her head, "And another glass of wine."

Nick raised his hand to catch the waiter's eye and as he approached asked, "Dessert menu, please."

Nick looked deeply into Muriel's eyes as she asked, "Are you always that calm, cool, and collected under pressure?"

He chuckled and held out a hand above the table, "As the adrenaline wears off I'll start shaking, I promise."

"So, how do you do that, be so kind and disarming at the same time?"

His chuckle continued, "A gift, I guess. In the middle of things it gets more difficult to perceive the promptings of the Holy Spirit, but I try to remain open to Him."

"Is that what it was like during the actual abduction?" she probed deeper. They ordered their desserts.

"I suppose," he answered her question after the waiter left. The desserts arrived. He looked down at his plate, "I feel like we should offer thanks again," he said jokingly.

Muriel smiled in response, "Be my guest."

Although he had been only kidding, he did take advantage of the opportunity. "Thank You for taking care of that situation. Be with Jarvis and help him find You through all of this." He looked down at his plate, "And thanks for this dessert, wow!" He brought a forkful of his chocolate extravaganza to his mouth, "What do you know about angels? Can they love?"

Her eyes widened, "What brings this up?"

"Just something I'm pondering and thought we could ponder together." He looked over her shoulder.

"Well, they worship, that would be an expression of love." She ate a spoonful of her custard.

"One point on the plus side," Nick added as he took a small notebook out of his pocket and began recording what they came up with.

"Is this a contest?" She squinted at him.

"No, just keeping track of our pondering. The fallen angels lusted after the daughters of men, that would be a kind of love." He jotted that down too. "Lust is just an emotion, neither good nor bad. It depends on what you are strongly desiring. Like Paul says in First Timothy three, 'If anyone aspires to the office of Bishop, he desires a noble task.' The word used there for desires is 'lusts.'"

It was Muriel's turn, "What about the angel that calls Gideon into service with, 'The LORD is with you, O mighty man of valor.' That sounds at least like respect."

Nick conceded, "Good point." He pondered a moment, "And the whole relationship with Uriel and those traveling to find the new born King that I describe in *The Magi and a Lady*, while fictitious, is based on fact. There seems to be some kind of relationship between them."

It was Muriel's turn again, "What about the kindness displayed to Lot and his family before the destruction of Sodom and Gomorrah? That would show a kind of compassion."

Nick was scribbling faster than eating his dessert, "Another good point. Hey, you're good at this."

She scrunched up her face, "You sound surprised?"

"Pleased would be closer to the target," he encouraged.

"And Gabriel's relationship to Mary at the time of the annunciation?" She chimed in again.

"Oh, yes. You wouldn't know this, but I once wrote and directed a short Christmas drama about that very thing. In working with the actor who was going to play Gabriel, I told him, 'Mary is so very special that when you first see her you are stunned and almost fall in love with her yourself.' He pulled it off perfectly. He stepped out from behind an object and saw her for the first time. He was shocked speechless. Gabriel shocked speechless!

It was quite memorable and also was beautiful. We should each get a point for that one." He paused, then continued, "A little diversion. Can a man love a woman passionately, intimately, without it being sexual?"

She had finished her dessert and took a slow drink of her wine, "Like Joseph had to do until Jesus was born?"

It was as if she had slapped him. "Yes, like that," he exclaimed and ate the last bite of his dessert. He whispered, "Did he kiss her?"

Muriel smiled coyly, "Ah, the age-old question of every teenage boy, 'How much physical affection can I show without going too far?' You might also wonder if he wanted her sexually, but knew he couldn't, shouldn't, and so didn't?"

"Hmmm, a question for another time. Coffee or a walk along the cliff?" and he took a drink of water.

"Regardless, I need to visit the Powder Room," and she stood up.

Nick stood too and motioned to the waiter for the check. He paid the check, visited the restroom himself, and was waiting with her wrap when she exited the Powder Room.

She laughed lightly, "I guess it's a walk?"

"Yes, I guess it is," and he offered her his arm. Before she took his arm she put on her wrap. Then she took his arm and gave it a slight squeeze.

It was a perfect evening for a stroll along the cliff. The night was crystal clear, not too crisp, and the stars were out in all of their glory. At its end there was a viewpoint that stretched out over the cliff to look dangerous, but wasn't. They stood there, arm in arm, their other hands resting on the rail and just soaked it in.

He began quietly, "Remember in Numbers twenty-five, after Balaam and Balak had led Israel into sexual immorality and how Phinehas, the priest, took action? He picked up a spear and put an end to it and the plague. God said that, 'He had been jealous with my jealousy, or zealous with my zeal.' God was so touched by the passion that Phinehas displayed that he gave him an 'everlasting priesthood.' That was a positive passion that was expressed even violently. Hmmm."

Musingly she responded, "Like that interesting verse in Matthew, '*The kingdom of God suffers violence and the violent take it by force.*'"

Nick smiled, "Yea, like that one, or Jesus cleansing the temple. Hmmm, we live in a funny world, where love often seems weak and puny, when it ought to be a powerful force for good."

Muriel nodded as she continued to ponder the effects of a powerful love. Their drive home was spent mostly in silence.

Chapter Twenty-Five: Freddy's Young Friend

Julie had just brought Nick his breakfast when Freddy walked in the door accompanied by a young man. "Thanks, Julie." She of course responded, "My pleasure," with a smile.

"Freddy, would you and your friend like some breakfast?" It was starting out to be a good day.

Freddy walked up to the table, "I would like to introduce you to my son, Kevin. I believe that he already knows you from school."

Kevin added his, "Hi, Mr. Grant."

"I do know Kevin, but I did not realize that he was your son. I hadn't made the connection. Sit down and let me buy you breakfast." The day kept getting better. They both sat down. Nick brought up the App on his phone and handed it to Freddy, who handed it to Kevin with, "Not very smart-phone savvy, remember?" After he finished ordering, Kevin handed the phone back to Nick.

"Nick, you will be pleased to know that I traded my handgun in for a bunch of fly-fishing equipment!" Freddy seemed quite pleased with himself.

Nick felt a shiver of excitement run up and down his spine, "So, you are a fly fisherman?"

Freddy grinned, "Yes, but it was time for some new gear. Well, new to us. Do you fly fish?"

Nick answered excitedly, "I do, and my brother-in-law taught me how to tie my own flies. We used to save all our prescription pill bottles during the year and give them to him. He would tie flies, put them in the pill bottles, and give them to kids when he taught them to fish."

Freddy looked off to the right, "What a great idea."

Nick winked at Kevin, "So, how much does he know about what I teach you?"

Kevin winked back, "I told him he was a Dreamer and he responded, 'Tell me something I don't know.' I then told him that it wasn't wrong to be impulsive, it was just part of who he is. He laughed at that."

Nick added, "But it doesn't make it less true does it? And what did you tell him about yourself?"

Kevin looked over Nick's left shoulder, "That because I'm a Detailer he should be especially glad that I keep my room clean and neat."

"Except that it is not hard for you to do that, you do it naturally."

He looked at Nick, "He still should be glad." He chuckled, "I also told him that he isn't messy, he just organizes stuff in piles." Freddy pushed him in the shoulder lovingly.

"So," Nick questioned, "what brings you to my office?"

Freddy looked down at the table, "I was wondering if you'd be interested in mentoring my son?"

Nick thought he heard a distant bell chime, but tried not to answer too eagerly, "What did you have in mind?"

"I know you have a lot you could share with him that I never could. My life has been a little," and he searched for the right word, "distracted." Freddy wasn't ashamed, just honest.

Nick thought a moment, prayed a quick prayer under his breath and responded, "How about breakfasts on Saturdays, here at my desk?"

Freddy turned to his son, who said, "I would really like that, Mr. Grant."

Nick smiled, "You know that I won't go easy on you just cause you're the son of a friend?"

Kevin smiled too, "I was afraid of that."

"Do you have an iPad besides the one the school gives you?" Nick inquired. Kevin shook his head. "I think I have an old one at home. I'll put a copy of my Christmas novel on it and we can start by discussing it. Let's say the Preface and the first three chapters by next Saturday? Does that sound okay?"

Kevin nodded.

"Great, check with me Monday at school. Now, Freddy, how's the job going?"

Freddy placed his hand on the table as he began, "It's actually going quite well. I have finished my probationary time, so have gotten my first pay raise." He pushed an envelope across the table. Nick looked at the envelope. "I'd like to pay you back for the money you lent me to get started in this new life."

Nick pursed his lips, "It wasn't a loan. It was a gift. Bank it for now and ask Him," and Nick pointed upwards, "what you should do with it."

Freddy reluctantly took it back and looked at his son who said, "See Dad, I told you. I have been through his Finance class, remember." They smiled at each other.

Later that morning Nick called the police station. A woman answered the phone, "Franklin PD, home of Franklin's finest."

Nick took a deep breath, "I'm trying to get in touch with Officer Donnelly."

She replied, "He's out on patrol right now. Could I give him a message?"

"Sure, could you tell him that Nick Grant called?" Nick stated.

There was a pause on the other end of the line, "Not the Nick Grant that foiled the abduction of that young girl?"

Nick, embarrassed, responded, "Yeah, that Nick Grant."

"Wow, a pleasure to meet you. What can we do for you?" she said excitedly.

Another deep breath, "I was wondering if it were possible to get a hold of the address of Samantha, the young girl who's abduction I foiled? I'd like to check and make sure she's okay. A trauma like that can be pretty devastating."

She questioned, "You teach at the high school too, don't you?"

It was beginning to sound like an interrogation, "Yes, psychology and life skills.

"Well, I can't do what you have asked, but I can pass your phone number to her mom, Mrs. Little, in case she wants to thank you," she left him hanging there.

"Okay, if that's the best you can do."

Later that day Samantha's mother called Nick. During their conversation she gave him their address and their phone number. He still felt an urge to see her, so he asked if he could. She said yes. So, he grabbed his coat and headed for Salishan, a poorer part of town.

The homes had been remodeled a few years ago, so they weren't as bad as Nick remembered, but you could tell from the cars and lack thereof that the clientele hadn't changed much. He found the address, half of a duplex. As he parked, he wondered if his shiny new electric car would still be there when he returned for it. He walked up to the door, said another short prayer, and knocked. The porch light came on and the door opened a crack to reveal a bedraggled, poorly dressed woman in her thirties.

"Mrs. Little, I'm Nick Grant."

She interrupted him, "I know who you are. I've seen you on TV." She paused, "I'm Terri."

He was unsure of what lay behind her remark about his being on TV, "Could I see your daughter?" She humphed, stepped back and opened the door.

Still speaking with an edge to her voice, "I'll go get her."

Samantha came running out of the back of the house squealing, "Mr. Nick, Mr. Nick!" And she ran into his arms. She just held him for the longest time, but finally let him go.

Nick looked back at her mother, "Could I take you all out to lunch?" He smiled his best smile, "I have a table reserved at Chick-fil-A."

Mrs. Little finally broke a slight smile, "That would be nice, let me get my shoes."

Chick-fil-A was usually very busy during the lunch hour, but fortunately Nick had called ahead and told them he was coming and they got there a little early and before the main lunch rush.

They walked in and Billy was sitting at Nick's table, so no one else would. He got up as the three of them approached, "Little late, is this second breakfast?" Billy joked.

Nick chuckled back, "My toes are hairy like a Hobbit too. Thanks for holding my table."

"What can I get started for you?" He had his drive-thru tablet in his hands.

"Thanks, Billy. We can just order off the App," Nick responded.

"Wait a sec, I've got something new for you," and he headed for the counter. Nick, Terri, and Samantha sat at Nick's table. Billy returned and handed him a sheet of paper, "Our take-out menu."

Nick looked at it. The front listed most of what was available for breakfast and the back for lunch. "What a great idea. That should help people be ready to order or even pre-order. Thanks." Billy went outside to help take orders in the drive-thru lane.

Nick placed the lunch menu between Terri and Samantha. They went through it and entered their order on the App on his phone. Even though the restaurant was pretty busy their order was brought to the table in only minutes.

Julie placed it on their table with a, "A little late for breakfast, Mr. Nick."

"Yeah, I know, thanks, Julie," and he waited.

He was not disappointed, "My pleasure." She delivered it with a smile.

They had a nice lunch and Nick got to know Samantha's mother, Terri, a little better. She had a tough upbringing, being raised by a single parent herself. She had gotten into drugs because of her husband, but he left when Samantha was born. She continued to have problems with drugs until she had gotten clean six months ago. Now she was trying for all she was worth, holding down two waitress jobs to make ends meet, but pretty much living paycheck to paycheck. That's why she had been gone the fateful day of the foiled abduction. Samantha had noticed they were out of a few things, knew where the grocery money was kept, and went to pick up some macaroni and cheese. It should have been okay. They knew her at the store and probably thought the guy who tried to pick her up was just her dad. It was probably just a simple collision of unfortunate circumstances, but then Nick came to the rescue. Now the man responsible had been caught and it appeared that everything was heading in the right direction again.

Nick asked silently for permission and then asked, "What other skills do you have besides waitressing?"

Terri looked down at the table, "I barely graduated from high school, ran the front counter at an ice cream joint, waitressed at a variety of places. That's about it."

Nick summarized, "So, you are personable, handle the public well, work a variety of hours, things like that?"

Terri smiled, "Yes, it doesn't sound so bad when you put it like that."

Nick smiled too, "Would you be open to a change, something full time, that might pay more?"

Now she was excited, "Yes!"

Nick chuckled, "Don't get your hopes up too much, but let me nose around." He looked at Samantha, "How about an ice cream cone?"

They said, "Yes!" nearly in unison.

Back in Salishan, Nick walked them to their door and Terri thanked him for lunch. She still licked her ice cream cone, "Thank you, that was very special," as she unlocked the door.

Samantha hugged him tight for a long time then added her, "Thank you, Mr. Nick." She stood in the doorway and waved as he drove off.

Chapter Twenty-Six:
Sunday School's Hero

When Nick walked into his Sunday School class he was stunned. It was standing room only and there wasn't much room left to stand.

Someone shouted from the back, "Mr. Grant, we hear that you're a hero." That was followed by applause.

Nick blushed, "I think you guys are trying to embarrass me. Well, good luck with that."

The class laughed.

"I suppose this concerns the attempted abduction that was foiled at the grocery store?" Nick paused and looked around the class, "Well, it was a pretty dangerous thing to do. It should have been prefaced with 'Don't try this at home.'"

More laughter filled the room.

"But seriously, the young girl was taken home and the perpetrator apprehended. I know, it was potentially very dangerous, and I would not suggest that you do the same except under a strong leading of the Holy Spirit. Now, can we get on with class?"

There was a general head nodding and his students began to settle in.

"Most all of you know my views on prayer. It is supposed to be conversation with God. It has nothing to do with closing your eyes, bowing your head, and folding your hands. One of you might say, 'But it helps me focus, concentrate.' I would answer that you don't need to do that to talk to me. Another might say, "It's a sign of respect." and again I would say," and he waited for them to say, "You don't do that when you talk to me."

Nick began again, "If you need something to help you focus or show respect," and he placed an empty chair next to where he stood, "pretend He's sitting there. He's everywhere, so He could very well be sitting there. Meredith, would you like to open class in prayer?"

He looked at her and she actually winked at him. He was startled for a second, but then she looked towards the chair and began, "Jesus, thanks for this time and for what You have for us. Help us to be listening, receptive," and she smiled, "and ready to respond. Amen." There was a chorus of other "Amens."

"How many of you see me as a pretty 'upbeat' kind of guy?" He scanned the room as virtually all the hands went up. "Well, that's good to know," and he smiled, "There is, however, something that should sober us all to the core. I ran across one of them this last week. Paul says in First Timothy one fifteen,

'It is a trustworthy saying and deserving of our full acceptance, that Jesus Christ came into the world to save sinners, of whom I am the greatest.'

"Now, that doesn't seem like such a big deal. Paul was a great sinner. He had at one time persecuted the church! But as I read the last part again slowly. It says, "of whom I AM the greatest.' Paul was speaking in the present tense. Not that I was a great sinner, but still am. Another pastor put it this way,

'If the biggest sinner you know isn't you, then you don't know yourself very well.'

Wow, it's pretty sobering when you truly realize how great a sinner you really are. Scripture says, *'For all have sinned and fallen short of the glory of God.'*

And again, *'For I know that in my flesh there dwells no good thing.'*

"Those are probably not the verses you have posted on your bathroom mirror or hanging on the refrigerator door, but they are none-the-less true. If we really believed this was true, how would it change us?"

From the middle of the class Nadine slowly raised her hand, "Yes, Nadine."

Nadine spoke hesitantly, "I think that we would be less arrogant, less confident in ourselves."

"Yes, thank you," and Nick finished her thought with, "and perhaps more dependent on Him and His grace." He was pointing upward. Nick looked at his watch. "So, this week, not only ponder your own sinfulness, but receive more of His grace. Nadine would you pray?"

Nadine looked toward the vacant chair, as a smile covered her face, "Thank You for giving us something to ponder, but thank You more for giving us Your Grace to receive. Amen."

Nick added, "See you next week."

In the morning service, Tom spoke, coincidentally, on "The Vastness of God's Grace."

As Nick and Muriel walked to his car he asked, "Lunch?"

Muriel responded, "That would be nice."

He shook his head from side to side, "No, I mean, where would you like to have lunch?"

She smiled as he opened the door for her, "I know what you meant, you choose," and got into the car.

Nick smiled, "I'm feeling like a hamburger,"

She interrupted him, "And what does a hamburger feel like?"

He just shook his head and continued, "fries, and a shake. How about Wendy's?"

Muriel smiled back, "Suits me."

They sat there nursing their shakes when Nick said, "There's only one thing wrong with this shake."

She looked up, "What's that?"

"It tastes like more, and they don't do free refills on shakes."

She chuckled, "Life is tough, isn't it?"

Nick decided to broach the subject he had been thinking about for a while. "What helped you the most in dealing with your grief over the loss of your husband?"

She looked at the table and then back up at him, "That's a sobering thought," and she paused. "I think the sale of the house. There was just too much around that reminded me that he was gone."

"Ah," and he pondered her answer, "but I really like my house. Although it is way too much for me to keep up. Besides, I will only be moving next door." He took a deep breath, "I think I am ready to put it on the market."

Muriel sighed empathetically, "Do you need any help moving?"

He smiled weakly, "Naw, I am pretty well finished with that. I would appreciate if you took a look at how I will have it staged though."

Her smile returned, "It would be 'my pleasure.'"

Nick laughed, "That's what they say at the other place."

Nick put the house on the market, and he had three offers that first week. It had recently become a seller's market so it became a bidding war between the three potential buyers. The final offer was thirty thousand dollars over Nick's asking price and belonged to a young family with two children all of whom had fallen in love with the place. The husband taught at the local community college and had heard of Nick's high school teaching. The wife had a green thumb and had promised to keep up the beautiful landscaping. It had been a win-win for them all. What had really surprised the new family was that when they went to sign the papers Nick had revised the price back to their originally offered price. He said that he was that pleased to have them as his new neighbors and to consider it as his gift to them for purchasing his former home. The couple had cried and then embraced him.

Chapter Twenty-Seven:
Opening the Church Library

As always, Tom's message was entertaining and yet pregnant with meaning. He ended with his usual challenge, "The only way the world will be transformed is if we are transformed first. So, be transformed by the renewing of your mind and then go out there and lead others to Christ. Please stand," and he paused while the congregation did. "We have a special treat for you this morning," and he looked at Nick's form hurrying towards the back of the congregation, "No, Nick did not bring in brownies from Chick-fil-A. They would be day-old, since they aren't open today."

A slight chuckle rippled through the congregation.

"Today is the grand opening of our new church library. Located to the right, as you leave the sanctuary, in rooms 224 and 225. There you will find quite a good initial collection of Christian literature from fiction to theology. As a special today, we are featuring a number of copies of Nick's own Christmas novel, 'The Magi and a Lady.' So, go check it out and have a great week."

Tom normally stood at the sanctuary's entrance and greeted folks as they left, but this morning he hurried to room 224 to be a part of the ribbon cutting ceremony. Tom, Nick, Ruth, Nichole, and Muriel stood before the door to room 224 which now sported a "Church Library" sign above the door. A number of the congregation stood in the hallway awaiting the library's formal opening. A red ribbon stretched across the doorway.

Tom took command of the situation with, "Please join me in prayer. Lord Jesus, thank you for the hard work that has gone into the preparation of this library, the donation of the initial books, and all that You have planned for this expression of our vision and ministry. May it all be for Your glory and praise, Amen." There were a number of other "Amens" voiced.

Nick handed the scissors to Ruth and Nichole, who cut the ribbon together, which was followed by polite applause.

Ruth addressed the small crowd, "Just inside to the right you will find the counter where one of us will usually be present. On the counter are two computers which you can use to both search for books and check out books. Each book has a QR code that you scan to bring up a simple menu for you to add your name, phone, and email. Books may be checked out for thirty days, normally renewable once. In room 225 there is a couch and arm chair for book browsing and a table for studying that may also be used for meetings. Are there any questions?" Ruth fielded a couple of questions and then folks were allowed into the library.

Both Nick and Ruth went to behind the counter. Ruth helped people check out books and answer other library-directed questions. Nick had the few copies of his Christmas novel on the counter and answered general questions about it. He also mentioned that he was working on his next one, the one he affectionately called "The Gospel According to Nick."

The morning proved quite productive. Not only did they check out all three copies of Nick's novel, but nearly twenty other books as well; including Tolkien, CS Lewis, George McDonald, E Stanley Jones, and some commentaries on the Epistles. The check-out process that seemed a little cumbersome at first, proved to be both fast and efficient. They all decided to go out to lunch together at Wendy's.

They sat, trays in front of them, as Nick began, "Well, that was pretty exciting for an opening."

Ruth joined in, "Yes, things went really well."

Nichole said, "I thought it might feel crowded with all the people, but actually, it didn't."

Muriel added, "And not a hiccup in the melee."

"Muriel, you want to bless our lunch?" Nick asked.

"Sure. Thanks for a great opening day, a great group of people, and even though it isn't Chick-fil-A, a great place to eat." They all shook their heads.

Chapter Twenty-Eight:
Cleveland High and Jarvis

When Jarvis was arraigned in court he pleaded guilty to attempted child abduction. When asked if he had ever abducted a child, his lawyer had counseled him that he didn't need to answer the question, so he had replied, "No comment." When asked if he had ever molested a child, his lawyer counseled him the same and he answered the same. He had undergone an evaluation by a psychiatrist and was found to be sane and no threat to himself or others. His court date was set to be in two weeks, and he was sent back to the county jail.

Nick called the jail to see if he needed to schedule an appointment to visit Jarvis. He had intended to visit him after school that Monday. They directed him to the Correctional Institution's website to find the procedure and requirements in order to have a successful visit.

Things at Cleveland High had returned to normal. Nick found no "hero" scrawled on the whiteboard when he entered the class. He breathed a sigh of relief.

"Okay, we have lots to cover. Turn in your book to page fifteen." Nick referred to the book, "You are Incredible" by Derrick Brinkman, that he had been privileged to discover so many years ago. He had been trained as a facilitator in its processes and was then allowed to teach from it at the high school level, as long as each student had a copy of the book. "Someone read the quote at the top of the page."

Jack stood up holding his book, "Your altitude will be determined by your attitude."

Before Jack could sit back down, Nick asked him, "And Jack, what does that mean to you?"

Jack smiled sheepishly, "I must admit that I have read ahead." He chuckled as he looked down at the book, "I would say that it means, that how high you rise in the organization, how far you go at work or in life in general, depends largely on how you approach things: your mindset, your values, your beliefs, your commitment, or in a word, your attitude."

Nick smiled in return, "Wow! Maybe I should trade places with Jack for the day."

There was light laughter throughout the classroom.

"A great way to start. Thank you Jack. So, let's define attitude." Nick looked at his copy of the book, "Your attitude is the direction to which you lean. You lean towards something, or you lean away from it. Regardless, you need to ask yourself, 'How is my current attitude impacting my current performance in this area of my life? If you want to change your performance, you need to change your attitude.'" He closed the book. "I want you to move into your personality quadrants, reread the chapter, and amongst your groups develop a list of how you can change your attitudes. Go!"

Nick sat in the waiting room of the County Jail waiting for his opportunity to visit Jarvis. He was surprised at all of the indignities that they put you through as a visitor. They treated you as an accomplice to the planned escape of the prisoner you were about to visit. After signing in, depositing all his belongings and everything in his pockets into a locker, including his coat and shoes, they did give him a package of disposable slippers. At least they stretched to fit Nick's size thirteen feet. Then there was the full-body scanner, which beeped because Nick forgot about the screw he had in his foot from when he broke it running. They patted him down and scanned him by hand. Then he was escorted to the waiting room.

While he was there for ninety minutes, Nick reread the first five chapters of the new book he was writing. Having published his Christmas novel he had felt led to continue the story with what was becoming what he affectionately called, "The Gospel according to Nick." The attending officers had paged through it to make sure he had nothing hidden in the pages. They didn't seem impressed that he was a published author. Finally, they called his name and escorted him to another room, where Jarvis sat handcuffed to the table. He tried to stand, then sat back down.

"Are they treating you okay?" Nick inquired sincerely.

Jarvis shrugged. "They think I'm a child molester," he stated despondently.

The guard said roughly, "Half an hour," and closed the door behind him.

Nick dug deeper, "So, what were your intentions that day?"

Jarvis looked down at the table, "I'm not really sure. She just looked so alone in that huge grocery store, wandering the aisles. I asked her who she was with and she mumbled, 'No one,' looking at the floor. It was just on impulse that I grabbed her hand and said, 'Come with me.' I guess I scared her."

"Where were you taking her?" It seemed logically the next question.

He looked slowly up from the table, "I'm not sure, I think I was just taking her to my car to find out where she lived and take her home."

"Were you armed that day? You reached in your coat under your left arm.? Nick hoped this was helping them both.

"Yes, I have a concealed weapon carry permit. I have worked private security after the Army." Now he looked Nick straight in the eye.

"And why did you reach for the gun?" Nick asked the next logical question.

"Old habit, I guess. You sort of caught me off guard. I didn't know who you were. It all happened so fast. Then I realized that you thought I was abducting her, so I got out of there." It seemed reasonable.

"And the whole thing at the restaurant?" Nick kept probing.

"Well, when it all went viral, you the hero and all, I guess I got angry." He looked down at the table again.

"Angry enough to kill me?" As usual, Nick's confidence was unnerving.

"That was just a threat. Fortunately, you are a much better man that I am. Maybe you deserve to be seen as the hero." He played with his handcuffs. "When you forgave me, it sort of took the wind out of my sails."

Nick sighed, "Well, I'm glad something interrupted where things were going." They both sat for a moment, "Changing the subject, have you ever read the Bible?"

Jarvis looked up, startled, "Why would you ask me that?"

Nick passed him the binder he had brought with him, "I'm sort of writing my own version. Call it 'The Gospel according to Nick,'" and he chuckled.

"You can do that?" It sounded like something that might be wrong.

Still chuckling lightly, "Yup, I wrote my version of the wisemen finding Jesus in Bethlehem and felt I was supposed to continue the story. I thought you might find it interesting."

"So, it's fiction?"

"Well," Nick paused, "The story is true, but my version of it is somewhat fictionalized."

Jarvis cocked his head to the side. "That is interesting. So to answer your original question, we used to read the Bible when I was growing up, but that was a long time ago."

"What happened? Why'd you stop?"

Jarvis returned to checking out the table top. "Mom remarried and he was abusive. He molested my sister, and I got beat up repeatedly for trying to intervene. As soon as I could, I left home.

I took my sister with me, but she didn't do well on the streets. She got into drugs and overdosed. I joined the Army to see the world, haha. I never even got out of the country." He was back to playing with his cuffs.

"What happened after that?" Nick inquired softly.

"I got hooked on pot in the Army. While doing private security after I got out, I tried to steal some money from the wrong guy, to support my habit. He shot me. When I got out of the hospital, I was out of a job."

The guard poked his head in the door, "Five minutes."

"When you were reading the Bible, did you ever meet Jesus?"

Jarvis looked up, "Huh?"

Nick continued, "You were created to know Him. Would you like to?"

Curious, Jarvis responded, "How?"

"Well, He is the God of the Universe," Jarvis looked at the table," so He's here. You just can't see Him." Jarvis looked up. "But you can talk to Him just like you talk to me."

"What do I say?" Jarvis asked sheepishly.

"Hello, would be good," Nick chuckled. "Then there are two things you need to accomplish. First, let Him take away the wrong that stands between the two of you, and second, let Him reconnect you to Himself as you were always intended to be."

"Do I need to bow my head, fold my hands, and close my eyes?"

Nick chuckled again, "Do you do that when you talk to me?"

Jarvis added his chuckle nervously, "No."

"Then just talk to Him. Pretend He's sitting right here," and Nick touched the back of the chair next to him.

Jarvis began slowly, "Jesus, hello. That sounds a bit strange," he paused. "Please take away the wrong that stands between us." He took a deep breath. "And reconnect us like we were always meant to be." He stopped. "I don't feel any different."

"That's okay, it's not about feelings. It's…"

But he didn't finish the sentence because of Jarvis' reaction. Jarvis had taken a deep shuddering breath accompanied by an, "Ah…" Then an, "Is that Him?"

Nick looked thoughtfully into the corner of the room, "I think so." Suddenly they were interrupted by the guard, "Time's up!"

"Read what's in the binder. I'd like to know what you think. I'll drop back in a few days." He pointed to the binder, Jarvis nodded, picked up the binder, and the guard led him out of the room.

Nick had no idea that would be the last time he saw Jarvis. He called the jail a few days later to find out that one of the other inmates had killed him for being a child molester. They didn't believe in "innocent until proven guilty." Nick sat at his desk and a tear trickled down his cheek followed by a few others. He sincerely hoped that his wife and daughters would introduce themselves to him in heaven. He had to leave it at that.

Chapter Twenty-Nine: Struggling On

"*Sometimes it seems that heartache and pain have decided to follow me.*" Nick mused. He recalled people in his past that had seemed to be 'trouble magnets.' He hoped that he wasn't becoming one of them. His phone rang. He was almost afraid to answer it, but he did any way, "How may I help you?"

"Is this Nick Grant?" the voice asked.

"Speaking." It was sad that there were now scams that recorded your voice, so that if you answered a question with a "Yes" they could add your "Yes," to something else, like "Would you like to buy 'X.'"

"This is Cheri Gardener at Child Protective Services. We have your name on record as the alternate contact for Samantha Little. Samantha Little's mother has died of an apparent overdose of drugs and we have taken the child into custody. She's asking for you"

Nick closed the lid on his laptop. "Where are you located? I'll be right there." They gave him the address, he quickly put on a tie, grabbed his coat, and was out the door in a flash.

They were on the fifth floor of the County City building. Because it was a government building it was quite a procedure, scanners and all, to just get in, not as extensive as the jail, but almost. On the fifth floor, he gave his name to a receptionist and took a seat. A smartly dressed young woman came out and called his name. She ushered him into a room where Samantha sat huddled in an arm chair in the corner. She looked up when the door opened, saw him, jumped to her feet and ran to his arms.

"It's okay kiddo, I'm here," but it wasn't okay. She burst into tears. He held her until the sobs subsided. She took a deep breath, then another and another.

She pulled a little away from him and looked up into his eyes, "Can I stay with you?"

Nick looked over at Miss, or maybe it was Mrs., Gardner, "Is that even possible?"

She responded, "We cannot discuss that with her in the room. It's policy," she said it emphatically.

Nick took out his keys and handed them to Samantha, "Will you be okay for a few minutes in here while I talk to, 'Is it Miss or Mrs.?'"

She said it was Miss.

"Miss Gardener?" He handed Samantha his keys.

She looked at them like, *"What are these for?"*

"It's a guarantee. I can't leave without them. So, I will definitely be back," and he winked.

She clutched them to her chest and sat back in the armchair.

Nick turned to Miss Gardner, "Okay, let's see what we can do." It took most of an hour to fill out all the paperwork, but when they were done the feeling that trouble had been following him seemed to dissipate like a spring fog when the sun bakes it into nothingness.

Samantha was placed in a temporary home. It took almost two months of home visits, various phone calls, and finally a court date, but just before Thanksgiving, he got the call from Miss Gardner. He was given the address and phone number of the home where Samantha currently stayed. If he dropped by the office to sign and pick up the final paperwork, he could go get her whenever he wanted. They would be expecting his call. He didn't have to be asked twice. He closed the screen of his computer and grabbed his coat almost before the phone responded with a dial tone. He called the home where Samantha was staying and told them he was coming over with a copy of the paperwork that would release her into his care.

Chapter Thirty: Kevin

Kevin sat across from him at his desk at Chick-fil-A. They had just finished breakfast and the "How have you been?" small talk.

Nick then asked, "So, how far have you gotten in *The Magi and a Lady*?"

Kevin looked down, smiling to himself. "I'm reading it a little slower this second time through. I wanted to get a feel for the whole thing first."

Nick's eyes widened, "You've already read it through once?"

"Yup."

Nick was pleasantly surprised, "Well, what did you think?"

Kevin paused, let him sweat a little, then he laughed, "I liked it."

"Whew," Nick exclaimed, "you had me going there for a minute. What stood out to you?"

"I think the soldier with the 'singing sword' is pretty cool and I like the 'Lady,' too."

"What did you like about Hannah?" Nick was really enjoying this. It validated his whole purpose for writing.

Kevin jumped in without a pause this time, "That she can fight with a sword, and talks to animals, too."

"What else?"

"That the star they followed was really an angel, Uriel the archangel. That possibility never occurred to me before."

Nick agreed, "Yeah, the whole 'followed a star' thing never made a lot of sense to me, but following an angel seemed to make perfect sense."

"I do have a question though," Kevin posed. "Once over the initial shock, they all seemed to treat Uriel like a regular person."

"Yeah," he waited for the other shoe to drop.

"Would it still be like that today?" Kevin added.

Nick responded, "I am reminded of the verse in the Scriptures, *'Do not neglect to show hospitality to strangers, for thereby some have entertained angels unaware.'* That would seem to indicate that at least some angels are walking around looking like men. Looking like strangers, but not strange," and he chuckled.

Kevin's eyes widened, "Have you ever met one? An angel?"

Nick smiled again, "Like my friend Jonathan says, 'I could tell you, but I'd have to kill you.'"

Kevin's eyes widened even more, "You have a friend who is an angel?"

"I didn't say that." He changed the subject, "Was there anything that you didn't like about the book?"

"The bad guys were pretty bad. Do you really believe that there are bad singing swords?" Kevin asked.

"According to the legend, yes. There is at least Lucifer's and the two swords that belonged to the archangels that rebelled with him." Nick wondered if Kevin had taken notes as he read the book.

"But Lucifer's isn't one of the original seven," Kevin said confidently.

"That is true, but maybe it was originally even specialer," Nick added, "I like that word, 'specialer.'"

Kevin looked at him quizzically, "I think you made up that word."

"I still like it," Nick stated. "That's an author's prerogative, to make up words."

Kevin smiled, "I think you just made that up too."

They both laughed.

"Did the book make you see God any differently?" Nick asked.

Kevin looked off into the distance, "Hmmm, I'll have to think about that."

Chapter Thirty-One:
Samantha Meets Muriel

It was difficult now for Nick to think of what life would be like without Samantha. She loved her own bedroom and they had turned the upstairs into an entertainment center with a large flat screen hooked up to a computer. They added an old comfy couch that turned into a full-sized bed. It was possible to use it for guests, but they hadn't had any yet.

Sam, his new nickname for her, now joined him at Chick-fil-A for breakfast each morning, six days a week, and was accepted by everyone as part of Mr. Nick's family. She soon met his friend Jonathan.

"So, this is the young lady that Mr. Nick rescued from the clutches of abduction?" Jonathan half joked.

Sam sat up a little taller, "Yes, that would be me."

His demeanor turned more somber, "I was sorry to hear about your mother."

She slumped a bit, "I know she wasn't trying to kill herself," her voice broke. Both Nick and Jonathan reached over and placed a hand on one of Samantha's.

"Yes, especially when she was doing so well at turning things around, building a future for you." Jonathan whispered.

She looked up wondering, *"How would he know that?"* and followed it with a, *"Nick must have told him."*

Attempting to lighten things up Nick spoke cheerfully, "I have a surprise for you,"

Just as he finished the door opened and in walked Muriel. "Here's my other good friend. Let me introduce you to Muriel. Muriel, this is Sam."

Muriel held out her hand, "A pleasure to meet you. I have heard lots about you, all good mind you," and Muriel chuckled. "What's it like living with the old guy," and she pointed to Nick.

Sam smiled broadly, "I didn't know life could be this wonderful."

"Yes, even amidst all the darkness and tragedy it can still be wonderful. We know that to be true." Muriel responded wistfully. "Do you like his little house?"

Sam looked at Nick, "Yes, I have a room all to myself, and we even have a big-screen for movies up in the entertainment room."

Muriel continued, "Did you know that he used to own the house next door? The gray one with the big chestnut tree?"

Sam shook her head.

"That's where he lived with his wife and two daughters before they died." Sam looked at Nick with wide eyes of surprise and shock.

Nick was a bit shocked too. "Maybe we should end the old family history lesson there for the day and return to happier things?"

But Sam wasn't quite ready to let things go. "You used to have two daughters?"

Nick sighed, "Yes, I did. That's one of the reasons I was allowed to take you in as your foster father. I had already raised two daughters."

"And they died?" There might have been a tear in Sam's eye.

Nick looked off over Sam's shoulder. "Yes, they died in an auto accident, along with my wife."

Sam reached out her hand, which Nick took. She drew it to her tear-stained face. "I'm so very sorry."

Nick sighed again, "It's okay, now I have you," and he tried a small smile. Then he snorted, "And there's Muriel."

Muriel's own eyes widened in surprise, seemingly being compared to Nick's wife.

Nick sat up, "Should we go see the polar bears at the zoo today?" It was like the clouds parted and the sun shown through. "Yes, let's do that!"

Muriel looked at him apologetically, "Am I invited?"

Nick gave a mock sigh, "I guess so," then turned to Jonathan. "You want to come too in case we need to be protected from stray pigeons?"

Jonathan seemed surprised they still realized he was there. "Are you sure that I won't take their side?" and he too laughed.

"Good, then it's settled." Looking still at Jonathan, "Do you want to leave your little electric car here and ride with us?"

Jonathan strung out his words in a long sigh himself, "I guess I'll leave it, just let me tell them at the desk."

"Muriel, do you want to ride with us too?" His glance moved towards her.

"Sure, I'll just move my car to the back lot and you can pick me up." She began to gather the remains of her breakfast, as did the rest.

On the way to the garbage machine, Nick announced, "Then we're off to our next adventure."

Chapter Thirty-Two: Sleepover

Nick and Sam sat at their favorite place for their favorite meal of the day, breakfast. Samantha had just finished her tater tots, "Nick, can I have a sleepover tonight at our house?"

Nick looked over her shoulder and out the front window of Chick-fil-A. "An interesting idea. How many of your friends were you thinking? Your bedroom isn't very large."

As he brought his eyes back to hers, she responded, "Only a couple of them from school."

He looked back away, as though listening, "Have I met them?"

She sighed, "I know what you're doing when you're looking over my shoulder. You're checking with Him."

Nick smiled, "That's okay, isn't it?"

Samantha smiled back, "Well, what did He say?"

Nick snickered a little, "He said, 'Ask her more questions.'"

She humphed, "He did not!"

Nick took a sip of his Coke Zero. "Well, not in those exact words."

She shook her head, then continued, "You've met Lucy Tanner, but not our friend Anna, and to answer your next question," she paused for emphasis, "everybody knows you, Mr. Grant the former high school teacher, so I'm sure it will be okay with their parents."

Nick furrowed his brow, "Any other questions I should be asking?"

She furrowed hers back, "I was thinking of six-thirty-ish, after supper, for a video in the upstairs, with popcorn, and maybe followed by root beer floats."

"Guess I can't say that you haven't thought this all out."

Samantha un-furrowed her brows and smiled again, "You sound surprised?"

"Nope." He raised a finger like she might have forgotten something. "Are we picking them up?"

She smiled broadly, she hadn't forgotten to think of this. "No, they will be delivered."

He raised his finger again, "And tomorrow?"

She mimicked looking over his shoulder, "After you buy them breakfast at Chick-fil-A, we'll take them home."

"Touche," and he lifted his cup. "Refills?"

She nodded and started to get up, picking up the tray of their wrappers and empty boxes. He grabbed her empty cup and headed for the counter, as she discarded their trash in the machine.

Nick and Samantha were sitting on their couch after supper when the doorbell rang. He answered it, "Mrs. Tanner, Lucy, and this must be Anna?"

Tonya Tanner answered, "Good evening, Mr. Grant. You're sure you're ready for this?"

Nick laughed, "I think so, come on in, ladies. I'll have them back about nine-ish in the morning, if that's okay?"

Tonya smiled, "Yes, that will be fine, assuming they get some sleep tonight."

The gals came in, Anna holding Lucy's arm tightly. Nick registered something odd but couldn't put his finger on it. Then it clicked, Anna was blind. Tonya turned and headed back to her car, got in, and waved at Nick as he waited on the porch until she was gone.

The gals were sitting next to Samantha on the couch when Nick returned to the living room. He sat in the arm chair next to them.

"If I understand the plan for the evening, you're going to watch a video to the tune of some popcorn, then we'll have some root beer floats? Is that the plan?"

They all nodded and Samantha added, "Yup."

"If I could ask a silly question, aren't you blind, Anna? How are you going to watch a video?" He tried not to make her feel bad. Anna sat closest to him on the couch.

She turned to look at him, almost as if she could see. "Yes, Mr. Grant, I am blind."

He interrupted her, "Nick, please call me Nick."

"Okay, Nick." It was difficult to tell that she was blind. There were only small nuances. "I was blinded in a fire when I was young, but even when I was in the hospital it would seem that sometimes I could see, spiritually. Then I found this." She pulled out of her blouse a large ruby, on a chain, encased in an intricately worked setting. Just then the doorbell rang again.

Nick turned towards the door, then back to Anna. "Wow! That is an incredibly beautiful pendant." He turned back towards the door, "Excuse me for a minute."

He opened the door and there stood his good friend, Jonathan. "Jonathan, what a surprise. Come on in. Wait a minute. How do you know where I live?"

Jonathan smiled, "The information's out there. You just have to know where to look."

Nick thought about that for a minute, then motioned him in. They walked back into the living room, "Samantha, you know Jonathan. Jonathan, this is Lucy and Anna," as he gestured to each of them.

Anna exclaimed, "He's an angel!"

Startled, Nick responded, "I have never been able to get him to admit to that. Why do you think he's an angel?"

Her voice filled with awe, "He's surrounded by an aura of the most beautiful soft light."

Unfazed, Jonathan retorted, "And you are wearing the Way Stone."

Her awe did not diminish. "How could you possibly know that if you were not an angel?"

As usual, he responded without acknowledging her question. "Let Nick hold the stone."

She held the ruby out to Nick as she leaned forward. He took it reverently and exclaimed, "It's warm."

Sam remarked, "It's been resting inside of her blouse against her skin, of course it feels warm."

Nick's eyes widened, "No, it's like it's almost alive," and awe washed over his face.

"What do you see, Nick?" Jonathan asked almost casually.

Nick did seem to be describing something he was definitely looking at, "I see a stream or a creek, with a pathway following alongside of it as it meanders through a forest. It seems to enter the mouth of a large cave."

"Yes, that is it," Jonathan added as though he could see it too. "And Nick, what is your middle name?"

Looking quizzically, like, *"What does that matter,"* he answered, "Jon."

The doorbell rang and Jonathan said, "I'll get it." He returned with Muriel and introduced her to Lucy and Anna.

Nick had finally let go of the pendant, yet still sat there wide-eyed. "Muriel, what are you doing here?"

She looked at him quizzically, "I'm not sure?" Then the lights went out.

Jonathan had turned out the lights, but the room was still filled from the soft glow of Anna's ruby. "Muriel, take Anna's pendant in your hand."

Muriel knelt before Anna on the couch and reached out her hand. Anna leaned forward until the stone fell into Muriel's hand. "I just heard the words, 'I will show you the way,' sung powerfully in my heart."

Jonathan continued, "Tell Nick your middle name."

She let go of the stone thinking, "*What?*" but said softly, "Mary," and it seemed a distant bell chimed in Nick's heart.

Nick exclaimed, "Mary, why didn't I know your middle name was Mary?" but then he thought, "*She probably doesn't know that my middle name is Jon, either.*"

Muriel lifted her eyebrows, "You never asked?"

Jonathan repeated his earlier question, "And your middle name, Nick?"

Nick looked at Muriel, "Jon." Now her eyes widened as though with some secret information.

Jonathan spoke, "And your stone Jon?" It was almost like Jonathan had slapped him. He sat there shocked. He hadn't thought about his stone for ages. He had found it in a lake so many years ago with a friend.

Jonathan spoke again, "Go get it." It wasn't a command, but it might as well have been.

Nick got up to fetch it and when he returned, he too knelt before the girls on the couch, reached out his right hand, and opened it palm upward to reveal a yellow brown amber, almost the size of his palm.

Jonathan again, "Mary, place your hand over Jon's." She did and her eyes widened as beneath her hand the stone pulsed with life. Jonathan continued, "Jon, you may kiss your bride," and Jonathan laughed out loud as Jon started leaning towards Mary as if he might.

"I was only kidding, Jon!" Then he began again more somberly, "These are only two of the stones. There are many other stones that will belong to many other individuals. You will find them all before you are led by the Way Stone and Anna to the cave you saw in the forest."

Just then, Jon's smart watched buzzed with a message, "*Check your cell phone.*"

"Something's wrong," he said as he pulled his phone out and hit the home button. He was greeted with another message that was loud enough that it filled the room. Everyone heard the sound of an alert, followed by:

"We interrupt to bring you this news breaking announcement." The voice changed, "The Triparteum council has just announced that Adonis Ashereem has been appointed chancellor and potentate!" There was a roar of applause and jovial shouting filling the background.

Everything as they knew it was about to change.

THE END

or
does the story continue in
Amidst the Stones of Fire?

More Titles by William Siems

Amidst the Stones of Fire
Out of the Sanctuary

The Chayeem Chronicles
The Magi and a Lady (Book One)
Hane and a Centurion (Book Two)
Zach and a Guy Named Joe (Book Three)

The Adventures of R'gal the Archangel
The Sword of Shenah (Book 1)
The Prince and the Soldier (Book 2)

Follow William Siems on Facebook

If you have enjoyed this book or other titles by William Siems, please tell your friends and write a review on Amazon. This is the best way for authors to sell more books.

About the Author

William Siems, "Bill" to his friends, seems to have started telling stories as soon as he could talk. His wife says he still tends to share the truth creatively and with a flair for the dramatic. He grew up in south Seattle and has lived in Tacoma, Washington since 1972.

He worked nine years in hospitals, completing half his RN education. If you had a heart attack, he says he could half save you. Bill joined the Boeing Airplane Company in 1979. The last 15 years of his 32-year career there he taught Employee and Leadership Development. Bill often developed and taught his own course material. This led to writing numerous short stories and dramas, culminating in his first published novel, *Amidst the Stones of Fire*, in 2017 and its sequel, *Out of the Sanctuary*, in 2018. A Biblical Adventure series followed, named *The Chayeem Chronicles*. It begins with the Christmas adventure, *The Magi and a Lady*, and the gospel adventures, *Hane and the Centurion* and *Zach and a Guy Named Joe*, a rewriting of the first part of the book of Acts. This book, *School Daze*, begins a new contemporary series and perhaps acts as a tie-in to his first apocryphal novel, *Amidst the Stones of Fire,* completing the circle, although a companion novel is in the works.

Now retired, Bill spends his time teaching, mentoring, writing, acting in community theater, and enjoying his family. Bill and his wife Nancy, of more than fifty-five years, live near their three children and seven grandchildren and one great grandchild.

If you can't find Bill in his office at Chick-fil-A writing his next book, then he is probably at home across the street playing with the neighbor's dog, Stacy, to whom he is Dogfather.

Made in United States
Troutdale, OR
09/07/2024

22560552R00106